THE PICTURE OF
DORIAN GRAY

THE PICTURE OF DORIAN GRAY

by

Oscar Wilde

(The "Lippincott's edition")

Published by Solar Books 2008

ISBN 978-0-9799847-8-5

First published 1890

This edition first published 2000

by

Creation Books

Cover illustration:

"Of a Neophyte, and How the Black Art Was Revealed unto Him
by the Fiend Asomuel"

by

Aubrey Beardsley (1893)

Design:

Tears Corporation

CONTENTS

INTRODUCTION
by
Jeremy Reed
5

THE PICTURE OF DORIAN GRAY
15

Appendix One
THE PREFACE TO THE 1891 EDITION
177

Appendix Two
CHAPTER XVI FROM THE 1891 EDITION
181

INTRODUCTION

Good books like good music travel underground to reach their audience. One could justifiably argue a case for Oscar Wilde's *The Picture Of Dorian Gray* comprising a blueprint for the subversive genre of fiction which in the 20th century has counted amongst its numbers the works of Jean Genet, William Burroughs and J.G. Ballard.

Wilde's belief that the artist should be imaginatively free of moral inhibitions and socially exempt from accounting for that freedom was to make him into an unrepentant literary outlaw. In writing what was to be the first attempt at an explicitly homosexual novel in English literature, and one in which criminality is celebrated at the expense of bourgeois ethics, Wilde was to take on the role of antagonist to Victorian moral constraint. With his novel attacked for its licentious forays into the sexual and drug underworlds, Wilde was to retaliate by writing to the editor of the *St. James's Gazette* in defence of his placing imagination over and above sterile conventions. "I am quite incapable" Wilde wrote, "of understanding how any work of art can be criticized from a moral standpoint. The sphere of art and the sphere of ethics are absolutely distinct and separate; and it is to the confusion between the two that we owe the appearance of Mrs Grundy, that amusing old lady who represents the only original form of humour that the middle-classes of this country have been able to produce."

The Wilde who was to serve as the progenitor of novelistic amorality and to provide a template for the likes of Jean Genet and William Burroughs to advance this expression, was by sensibility a man at odds with his class. Wilde had married Constance Lloyd largely for financial considerations, and prior to the publication of *The Picture Of Dorian Gray* in 1890, had been considered as little more than an imposingly colourful aesthete, and an affected former editor of *Woman's World*. But the real Oscar, by which I mean the courageously defiant rebel, the irreverent O.T.T. and outrageously camp raconteur, and the hedonist who shot his cells with absinthe and brandy was also a man who cruised the bars off Shaftesbury Avenue in pursuit of rent boys. Wilde was by nature attracted to illicit pleasures and to the night as the arena in which he lived out his fascination with the London underworld. Psychologically angular to the 19th century ideal of family, and ill-suited to heterosexual relations, Wilde discovered in the language, dress and sexual preferences of his gay fraternity a release from the social orthodoxy which he so despised. It was of course the experientially lived-out probe of these aspects of Wilde's nocturnal psyche which were to provide him with material for the writing of his dangerously confessional novel. It has been suggested that Wilde's attention to the Piccadilly meat-rack was first aroused by his coming into contact with rent boys soliciting outside Swan & Edgar's, while visiting the shop with Constance. Whatever the corresponding archetype in Wilde's libidinal fantasies, the indelible impression left on him by the sight of available trade was to inspire in him the impulsive recklessness of a sexual outlaw subjected to the vicissitudes of blackmail. Wilde's own fear of being exposed for living a double life was of course injected into the figure of Dorian Gray who serves as the fictional counterpart to Wilde's nocturnally authorised excursions into West End gay life. Wilde's mistake was to trust the largely uneducated boys with whom he consorted, and his innately generous character was to be ruthlessly exploited and in time ruined by his misplaced sense of gay camaraderie.

Dorian Gray was written in late 1889, and the novel was published on 20 June 1890, as pp3-100 of the July issue of *Lippincott's Monthly Magazine*. Although Wilde was to say of the novel, "I am afraid it is rather like my own life – all conversation and no action," and was subsequently to add six new chapters' to the text in the interests of narrative development for the book's British publication in 1891, the Lippincott edition encapsulates the quintessentially decadent Wilde.

Wilde had inherited from Walter Pater and John Ruskin his aesthetic credo of art-for-art's sake, and Wilde's adaption of the classic Hellenic ideal of homosexual love is something covertly, but forcefully compounded into the Lippincott edition of *Dorian Gray*. Of the love that Dorian has inspired in the artist Basil Hallward, Wilde approvingly comments:"It was such love as Michelangelo had known, and Montaigne, and Wincklemann, and Shakespeare himself." Apprehensive of being prosecuted for his convictions, Wilde qualified his thesis in *Dorian Gray* by using art as a sanctioning reference point. And in terms of the book's three central characters embodying aspects of the author's private psychology, Wilde explained to a correspondent: "Basil Hallward is what I think I am: Lord Henry what the world thinks me: Dorian is what I would like to be in other ages, perhaps."

The original 1890 version of *Dorian Gray* has become a bibliophilic rarity, and its republication in this centennial edition allows the reader the privilege of insighting Wilde at the optimal moment of his aesthetic achievement.

Although Wilde added chapters and invented the figure of James Vane as the retributive antagonist to Dorian for the novel's publication in book form by Ward, Lock & Co, in 1891, *Dorian Gray* in both its editions remains essentially a novel of ideas. In this respect Wilde precedes the method adopted by Marcel Proust in *Remembrance Of Things Past*, a conceptual epic in which narrative drive is replaced by textual divigations into the discussion of art, music, fashion, literature and aesthetics. Wilde, who as a metaphorical colourist was influenced by the Huysmans of *A Rebours*, an indebtedness instanced by Dorian's preoccupation with jewels, perfumes, fabrics and the instrumentation contributing to primitive music, had sniffed at the changes to come in revolutionizing the novel. Frustrated by the limitations in subject matter which had squeezed the 19th century British novel to a condition of pathological inertia, Wilde argued against a literature constrained by ideological protocol. The Wilde who created the convincily subterranean character of Dorian Gray, whose pact with unchanging youth is contingent on a life of increasing moral corruption was the critic who advocated pushing the subject matter of literature to the cutting edge. "Any attempt to extend the subject-matter of art," he wrote, "is extremely distasteful to the public; and yet the vitality and progress of art depend in a large measure on the continual extension of the subject-matter."

It is worth noting that Wilde's books were in large published by independent houses. *The Picture Of Dorian Gray* was rejected by Macmillans on account of its offensive nature, and was brought out by the small firm of Ward, Lock & Co, and Wilde was to come to rely on the maverick independent publisher, Leonard Smithers, for the publication of his later books. Wilde was in this and every other respect an uncompromising outsider.

That *Dorian Gray* has survived a century after its first publication as a novel which continues to get under the reader's skin, and to shock by reason of its disaffiliation from ethics is a vindication of Wilde's achievement in writing what has become an underground classic. That the book itself was prophetic of Wilde's eventual imprisonment and social disgrace has served to accentuate Wilde's significance as archetypal hero to outsider factions.

In psychological terms Wilde the man was of course the tripartite synthesis of Lord Henry, Basil Hallward and Dorian Gray. It has been variously claimed that the latter figure was modelled on the person of John Gray, a minor poet who Wilde picked up at the Alhambra in Piccadilly, but this is to point to a basis of erroneous character specifics, rather than to the imaginative chemistry at work in Wilde's creation. The character Dorian Gray was not only built out of the black stuff in Wilde's neurology, but as an underworld component of Wilde's psyche symbolized what Jung was to subsequently call the shadow. We all contain the latent potential to realise evil through our actions, or to pathologize it through breakdown states, and by addressing the psychic counterpart who lived at his core Wilde was to create one of the most durable characters in fiction. Dorian represents the criminal as suprahuman apotheosis, unkillable except by his own hand, and in the manner of Jean Genet's fictional heroes, unconscionably evil by way of celebrating his perverse indifference to society. The protagonist of Wilde's novel prefigures the metamorphic character of Divine in Genet's *Our Lady Of The Flowers*. And to advance his theory that transgression is a necessary, if not redemptive experiential state for the artist to encounter, Wilde has Lord Henry propose the notion that our ability to evaluate the meaning of life hinges on a typically Wildean paradox: "to cure the soul by means of the senses, and the senses by means of the soul".

One could argue that Wilde like his creation Dorian Gray was run to ground for daring to live out the realisation of his inwardly evolved philosophy. Imagination is always the dynamic that society as a unit fears and finds intolerable. "Jesus Christ is imagination," Blake wrote, and Wilde by the time he came to write *Dorian Gray* had adopted a corresponding belief in the truth of imagination as the modem communicating to a new society. Wilde perceived with intransigent perspicuity that the premises on which society is built are those of political corruption condoned by moral hypocrisy. Who else but Wilde would have dared to sardonically indict marriage as a social institution, by having Lord Henry deconstruct its principles in terms which are both misogynistic and anarchic. Wilde, with more than a hint directed at his personal life, has Lord Henry pronounce: "You seem to forget that I am married, and the one charm of marriage is that it makes a life of deception necessary for both parties. I never know where my wife is, and my wife never knows what I am doing. When we meet – we do meet occasionally, when we dine out together, or go down to the duke's – we tell each other the most absurd stories with the most serious faces."

Wilde's own private life observed a trajectory not so dissimilar from that described by Lord Henry, his gay proclivities and the coterie with whom he associated having him live increasingly in hotels or in rented accommodation. Although Wilde was companionable to Constance, and must have proved an ideal friend to her, he came increasingly during the years 1891–95 to be a fugitive to his attenuated marriage.

The Lippincott edition of *Dorian Gray* is overtly homoerotic, and it was on the advice of friends that Wilde excised much of Basil Hallward's explicitly homosexual expositions for the publication of the revised edition. Wilde was opening himself up to trouble when he has Basil Hallward profess outright love to Dorian Gray. How were a morally straitjacketed late 19th century society to interpret Basil's confession of love to Dorian? Wilde has the impassioned Hallward profess: "It is quite true that I have worshipped you with far more romance of feeling than a man usually gives to a friend. Somehow, I had never loved a woman. I suppose I never had time... Well, from the moment I met you, your personality had the most extraordinary influence over me. I quite admit that I adored you madly, extravagantly, absurdly. I was jealous of every one to whom you spoke."

The publication of Wilde's *Letters* in 1962 allow us to hear in Hallward's proclamation of gay love, the characteristic manner of expression by which Wilde invariably addressed his fraternity of male lovers and friends. Wilde as a person seems to have symbiosed aspects of a flamboyant hedonist with those of a sensual decadent, a cocktail calculated to antagonize British suspicion and hatred.

Edmund White has observed that most of Marcel Proust's female characters are in fact boys in drag. Wilde avoided gender-bending in *Dorian Gray*, but his propensity to effeminize Dorian is such that his protagonist's features are described in a way which celebrates male beauty in diction usually accorded to the romantic idealization of women. In a memorable vignette, Wilde describes Dorian as a somewhat petulant blond. In Wilde's description: "The lad started and drew back. He was bare-headed, and the leaves had tossed his rebellious curls and tangled all their gilded threads. There was a look of fear in his eyes, such as people have when they are suddenly awakened. His finely-chiselled nostrils quivered, and some hidden nerve shook the scarlet of his lips and left them trembling."

Appended to the Lippincott text for the reissue of this novel are Wilde's self-vindicatory Preface to the 1891 Ward, Lock & Co. edition – first published in the March 1891 edition of *The Fortnightly Review* – together with Chapter XVI from the expanded book in which Dorian makes his unforgettably atmospheric journey to an opium den in Dockland, an example both of Wilde's textual additions and of his unrepentant urge to excavate society's lower seams. Wilde's evocation of Limehouse Chinatown at night and under driving rain presents an eerie clip of underworld geography. Through Dorian's attraction to a self-inclusive debasement, and through the relief he finds in mixing with junkies and criminals, Wilde implies that the inevitable counterpart to an over-applied aesthetic is ugliness and corruption. Dorian's excessively refined nature gravitates towards its opposite in the way that Wilde himself was to compensate for artistic elitism by an incurable attraction to lowlife. "People thought it dreadful of me," Wilde wrote, "to have entertained at dinner the evil things of life, and to have found pleasure in their company... It was like feasting with panthers. The danger was half the excitement."

Wilde broke class barriers by taking rent boys to fashionable restaurants like Kettners in Soho, or to the dining room at the Savoy, and the notoriety attached to such provocatory acts of ethical defiance were to be used as evidence against him in court. By 1895 Wilde's secret life had grown to be a documentary awaiting release.

In the Preface to the 1891 edition of *Dorian Gray*, Wilde had attempted to defend his notions of sexual and artistic freedom by writing: "There is no such thing as a moral or an immoral book. Books are well written, or badly written. That is all." He had also anticipated indignation being levelled at his work by stating: "Those who find ugly meanings in beautiful things are corrupt without being charming. This is a fault. Those who find beautiful meanings in beautiful things are the cultivated. For these there is hope." But in his attempt to forestall criticism of his novel Wilde had miscalculated. W.H. Smith refused to carry it, on the grounds that it was "filthy". The book was designated a "leperous distillment" of tainted love, and one critic concluded his review by saying, "I have read it, and except for the ingenious idea, I wish to forget it". Wilde had been marked by the expression of his aesthetic, and the authorities were never to forgive him this flagrant breach of morals. Wilde was in the eyes of his detractors to be identified with his subject, and so the conspiracy to ruin him increased in proportion to his contempt for the authorities. Wilde who was to console himself by consolidating his inner convictions acknowledged that, "On the whole, an artist in England gains something by being attacked. His individuality is intensified. He becomes more completely himself."

The post-*Dorian* years leading up to his arrest in 1895 were for Wilde the highpoint of a scandalous career. His plays brought him for a short time a controversial public profile, and the rapidly expended royalties derived from their success allowed Wilde to indulge to the full in an extravagantly sensual lifestyle.

It was soon after the publication of *Dorian Gray* in 1891 that Wilde was to meet the physical embodiment of Dorian's beauty in the spoiled, insolent and impetuously vindictive figure of Lord Alfred Douglas. The story of their unequal relationship and its disastrous consequences to Wilde is outside the scope of this essay; but it is interesting to note that Wilde in writing to a friend about his love for Bosie describes him in a language that corresponds to Basil Hallward's ecstatic praise of Dorian. "Bosie has insisted on stopping here for sandwiches," Wilde wrote to Robert Ross. "He is quite like a narcissus – so white and gold. I will either come Wednesday or Thursday night to your rooms. Send me a line. Bosie is so tired; he lies like a hyacinth on the sofa, and I worship him."

Wilde openly pursued his courtship of Douglas, and neither being faithful to the other, both procured boys from dubious sources. Wilde was to prove the subject of persistently invidious blackmail, and was finally to be the target of Bosie's obstreperously anti-homosexual father the Marquess of Queensbury. Queensbury had a reason to focus his anger on Wilde. Lord Alfred Douglas's brother, Viscount Drumlanrig, had been involved in a relationship with the prime minister, Lord Rosebery, and had subsequently committed suicide in 1893. Threatened by what he conceived to be a second homosexual scandal to his family, Queensbury resolved to ruin the offending Oscar and was instrumental to paying rough trade to perjure themselves in bringing evidence against Wilde in court.

That Wilde in a shambles of corrupt justice had to be tried three times before a conviction could be secured is now a part of the history of his fall. If Wilde the man was irreparably broken by being sentenced to two years hard labour, then the anarchic spirit informing *Dorian Gray* continues to inspire underground writing a century after his death. Wilde survived his release from prison in 1897 by less than three years, dying in part from the accumulative effects of an ear injury incurred during his time in Reading jail.

It seems appropriate that the republication of the Lippincott *Dorian Gray* should fall to the provenance of an independent publisher. I suspect that Wilde would view attempts by the establishment to repatriate him to revised standards as indicative of renewed hypocrisy. Conferring posthumous accolades on a writer victimized for being unreconciled to his times is a hollow gesture. It's easy to humour the dead; they can't answer back. Better far to remember the names of those friends who stood by Wilde in his last insupportable years. It is they who should be remembered, together with the powerful imaginative dynamic at work in this novel.

—Jeremy Reed
London, July 1999

THE PICTURE OF DORIAN GRAY

OSCAR WILDE

ONE

The studio was filled with the rich odour of roses, and when the light summer wind stirred amidst the trees of the garden there came through the open door the heavy scent of the lilac, or the more delicate perfume of the pink-flowering thorn.

From the corner of the divan of Persian saddle-bags on which he was lying, smoking, as usual, innumerable cigarettes, Lord Henry Wotton could just catch the gleam of the honey- sweet and honey-coloured blossoms of the laburnum, whose tremulous branches seemed hardly able to bear the burden of a beauty so flame-like as theirs; and now and then the fantastic shadows of birds in flight flitted across the long tussore-silk curtains that were stretched in front of the huge window, producing a kind of momentary Japanese effect, and making him think of those pallid jade-faced painters who, in an art that is necessarily immobile, seek to convey the sense of swiftness and motion. The sullen murmur of the bees shouldering their way through the long unmown grass, or circling with monotonous insistence round the black-crocketed spires of the early June hollyhocks, seemed to make the stillness more oppressive, and the dim roar of London was like the bourdon note of a distant organ.

In the centre of the room, clamped to an upright easel,

stood the full-length portrait of a young man of extraordinary personal beauty, and in front of it, some little distance away, was sitting the artist himself, Basil Hallward, whose sudden disappearance some years ago caused, at the time, such public excitement, and gave rise to so many strange conjectures.

As he looked at the gracious and comely form he had so skilfully mirrored in his art, a smile of pleasure passed across his face, and seemed about to linger there. But he suddenly started up, and, closing his eyes, placed his fingers upon the lids, as though he sought to imprison within his brain some curious dream from which he feared he might awake.

"It is your best work, Basil, the best thing you have ever done," said Lord Henry, languidly. "You must certainly send it next year to the Grosvenor. The Academy is too large and too vulgar. The Grosvenor is the only place."

"I don't think I will send it anywhere," he answered, tossing his head back in that odd way that used to make his friends laugh at him at Oxford. "No: I won't send it anywhere."

Lord Henry elevated his eyebrows, and looked at him in amazement through the thin blue wreaths of smoke that curled up in such fanciful whorls from his heavy opium-tainted cigarette. "Not send it anywhere? My dear fellow, why? Have you any reason? What odd chaps you painters are! You do anything in the world to gain a reputation. As soon as you have one, you seem to want to throw it away. It is silly of you, for there is only one thing in the world worse than being talked about, and that is not being talked about. A portrait like this would set you far above all the young men in England, and make the old men quite jealous, if old men are ever capable of any emotion."

"I know you will laugh at me," he replied, "but I really can't exhibit it. I have put too much of myself into it."

Lord Henry stretched his long legs out on the divan and shook with laughter.

"Yes, I knew you would laugh; but it is quite true, all the same."

"Too much of yourself in it! Upon my word, Basil, I didn't know you were so vain; and I really can't see any resemblance between you, with your rugged strong face and your coal-black hair, and this young Adonis, who looks as if he was made of ivory and rose-leaves. Why, my dear Basil, he is a Narcissus and you – well, of course you have an intellectual expression, and all that. But beauty, real beauty, ends where an intellectual expression begins. Intellect is in itself an exaggeration, and destroys the harmony of any face. The moment one sits down to think, one becomes all nose, or all forehead, or something horrid. Look at the successful men in any of the learned professions. How perfectly hideous they are! Except, of course, in the Church. But then, in the Church they don't think. A bishop keeps on saying at the age of eighty what he was told to say when he was a boy of eighteen, and consequently he always looks absolutely delightful. Your mysterious young friend, whose name you have never told me, but whose picture really fascinates me, never thinks. I feel quite sure of that. He is a brainless, beautiful thing, who should be always here in winter when we have no flowers to look at, and always here in summer when we want something to chill our intelligence. Don't flatter yourself, Basil: you are not in the least like him."

"You don't understand me, Harry. Of course I am not like him. I know that perfectly well. Indeed, I should be sorry to look like him. You shrug your shoulders? I am telling you the truth. There is a fatality about all physical and intellectual distinction, the sort of fatality that seems to dog through history the faltering steps of kings. It is better not to be different from one's fellows. The ugly and the stupid have the best of it in this world. They can sit quietly and gape at the play. If they know nothing of victory, they are at last spared the knowledge of defeat. They live as we all should live, undisturbed, indifferent, and without disquiet. They neither bring ruin upon others nor ever receive it from alien hands. Your rank and wealth, Harry; my brains, such as they are – my fame, whatever it may be worth; Dorian Gray's good looks – we will all suffer for what the gods have given us, suffer terribly."

"Dorian Gray? is that his name?" said Lord Henry, walking across the studio towards Basil Hallward.

"Yes; that is his name. I didn't intend to tell it to you."

"But why not?"

"Oh, I can't explain. When I like people immensely I never tell their names to any one. It seems like surrendering a part of them. You know how I love secrecy. It is the only thing that can make modern life wonderful or mysterious to us. The commonest thing is delightful if one only hides it. When I leave town I never tell my people where I am going. If I did, I would lose all my pleasure. It is a silly habit, I dare say, but somehow it seems to bring a great deal of romance into one's life. I suppose you think me awfully foolish about it?"

"Not at all," answered Lord Henry, laying his hand upon his shoulder; "not at all, my dear Basil. You seem to forget that I am married, and the one charm of marriage is that it makes a life of deception necessary for both parties. I never know where my wife is, and my wife never knows what I am doing. When we meet – we do meet occasionally, when we dine out together, or go down to the duke's – we tell each other the most absurd stories with the most serious faces. My wife is very good at it – much better, in fact, than I am. She never gets confused over her dates, and I always do. But when she does find me out, she makes no row at all. I sometimes wish she would; but she merely laughs at me."

"I hate the way you talk about your married life, Harry," said Basil Hallward, shaking his hand off, and strolling towards the door that led into the garden. "I believe that you are really a very good husband, but that you are thoroughly ashamed of your own virtues. You are an extraordinary fellow. You never say a moral thing, and you never do a wrong thing. Your cynicism is simply a pose."

"Being natural is simply a pose, and the most irritating pose I know," cried Lord Henry, laughing; and the two young men went out into the garden together, and for a long time they did not speak.

After a long pause Lord Henry pulled out his watch. "I am afraid I must be going, Basil," he murmured, "and before I go I insist of your answering a question I put to you some time ago."

"What is that?" asked Basil Hallward, keeping his eyes fixed on the ground.

"You know quite well."

"I do not, Harry."

"Well, I will tell you what it is."

"Please don't."

"I must. I want you to explain to me why you won't exhibit Dorian Gray's picture. I want the real reason."

"I told you the real reason."

"No, you did not. You said it was because there was too much of yourself in it. Now, that is childish."

"Harry," said Basil Hallward, looking him straight in the face, "every portrait that is painted with feeling is a portrait of the artist, not of the sitter. The sitter is merely the accident, the occasion. It is not he who is revealed by the painter; it is rather the painter who, on the coloured canvas, reveals himself. The reason I will not exhibit this picture is that I am afraid that I have shown with it the secret of my own soul."

Lord Harry laughed. "And what is that?" he asked.

"I will tell you," said Hallward; and an expression of perplexity came over his face.

"I am all expectation, Basil," murmured his companion, looking at him.

"Oh, there is really very little to tell, Harry," answered the young painter; "and I am afraid you will hardly understand it. Perhaps you will hardly believe it."

Lord Henry smiled, and, leaning down, plucked a pink-petalled daisy from the grass, and examined it.

"I am quite sure I shall understand it," he replied, gazing intently at the little golden white-feathered disk, "and I can believe anything, provided that it is incredible."

The wind shook some blossoms from the trees, and the heavy lilac-blooms, with their clustering stars, moved to and fro in the languid air. A grasshopper began to chirrup in the grass, and a long thin dragon-fly floated by on its brown gauze wings. Lord Henry felt as if he could hear Basil Hallward's heart beating, and he wondered what was coming.

"Well, this is incredible," repeated Hallward, rather bitterly – "incredible to me at times. I don't know what it means. The story is simply this. Two months ago I went to a crush at Lady Brandon's. You know we poor painters have to show ourselves in society from time to time, just to remind the public that we are not savages. With an evening coat and a white tie, as you told me once, anybody, even a stockbroker, can gain a reputation for being civilised. Well, after I had been in the room about ten minutes, talking to huge overdressed dowagers and tedious Academicians, I suddenly became conscious that some one was looking at me. I turned half-way round, and saw Dorian Gray for the first time. When our eyes met, I felt that I was growing pale. A curious instinct of terror came over me. I knew that I had come face to face with some one whose mere personality was so fascinating that, if I allowed it to do so, it would absorb my whole nature, my whole soul, my very art itself. I did not want any external influence in my life. You know yourself, Harry, how independent I am by nature. My father destined me for the army. I insisted on going to Oxford. Then he made me enter my name at the Middle Temple. Before I had eaten half a dozen dinners I gave up the Bar, and announced my intention of becoming a painter. I have always been my own master; had at least always been so, till I met Dorian Gray. Then – But I don't know how to explain it to you. Something seemed to tell me that I was on the verge of a terrible crisis in my life. I had a strange feeling that Fate had in store for me exquisite joys and exquisite sorrows. I knew that if I spoke to Dorian I would become absolutely devoted to him, and that I ought not to speak to him. I grew afraid, and turned to quit the room. It was not conscience that made me do so: it was cowardice. I take no credit to myself for trying to escape."

"Conscience and cowardice are really the same things, Basil. Conscience is the trade-name of the firm. That is all."

"I don't believe that, Harry. However, whatever was my motive – and it may have been pride, for I used to be very proud – I certainly struggled to the door. There of course, I stumbled against Lady Brandon. 'You are not going to run away so soon, Mr Hallward?' she screamed out. You know her shrill horrid voice?"

"Yes; she is a peacock in everything but beauty," said Lord Henry, pulling the daisy to bits with his long, nervous fingers.

"I could not get rid of her. She brought me up to Royalties, and people with Stars and Garters, and elderly ladies with gigantic tiaras and hooked noses. She spoke of me as he dearest friend. I had only met her once before, but she took it into her head to lionise me. I believe some picture of mine had made a great success at the time, at least had been chattered about in the penny newspapers, which is the nineteenth century standard of immortality. Suddenly I found myself face to face with the young man whose personality had so strangely stirred me. We were quite close, almost touching. Our eyes met again. It was mad of me, but I asked Lady Brandon to introduce me to him. Perhaps it was not so mad, after all. It was simply inevitable. We would have spoken to each other without any introduction. I am sure of that. Dorian told me so afterwards. He, too, felt that we were destined to know each other."

"And how did Lady Brandon describe this wonderful young man? I know she goes in for giving a rapid précis of all her guests. I remember her bringing me up to a most truculent and red-faced old gentleman covered all over with orders and ribbons, and hissing into my ear, in a tragic whisper which must have been perfectly audible to everybody in the room, some-thing like 'Sir Humpty Dumpty – you know – Afghan frontier – Russian intrigues: very successful man – wife killed by an elephant – quite inconsolable – wants to marry a beautiful American widow – everybody does nowadays – hates Mr. Gladstone – but very much interested in beetles: ask him what he thinks of Schouvaloff.' I simply fled. I like to find out people for myself. But poor Lady Brandon treats her guests exactly as an auctioneer treats his goods. She either explains them entirely away, or tells one everything about them except what one wants to know. But what did she say about Mr. Dorian Gray?"

"Oh, she murmured, 'Charming boy – poor dear mother and I quite inseparable – engaged to be married to the same man – I mean married on the same day – how very silly of me! Quite forget what he does – afraid he – doesn't do anything – oh, yes, plays the piano – or is it the violin, dear Mr. Gray?' We could neither of us help laughing, and we became friends at once."

"Laughter is not a bad beginning for a friendship, and it is the best ending for one," said Lord Henry, plucking another daisy.

Hallward buried his face in his hands. "You don't understand what friendship is, Harry," he murmured – "or what enmity is, for that matter. You like every one; that is to say, you are indifferent to every one."

"How horribly unjust of you!" cried Lord Henry, tilting his hat back, and looking up at the little clouds that were drifting across the hollowed turquoise of the summer sky, like ravelled skeins of glossy white silk. "Yes; horribly unjust of you. I make a great difference between people. I choose my friends for their good looks, my acquaintances for their characters, and my enemies for their brains. A man can't be too careful in the choice of his enemies. I have not got one who is a fool. They are all men of some intellectual power, and consequently they all appreciate me. Is that very vain of me? I think it is rather vain."

"I should think it was, Harry. But according to your category I must be merely an acquaintance."

"My dear old Basil, you are much more than an acquaintance."

"And much less than a friend. A sort of brother I suppose?"

"Oh, brothers! I don't care for brothers. My elder brother won't die and my younger brothers seem never to do anything else."

"Harry!"

"My dear fellow, I am not quite serious. But I can't help detesting my relations. I suppose it comes from the fact that we can't stand other people having the same faults as ourselves. I quite sympathise with the rage of the English democracy against what they call the vices of the upper classes. They feel that drunkenness, stupidity, and immorality should be their own special property, and that if any one of us makes an ass of himself he is poaching on their preserves. When poor Southwark got into the Divorce Court, their indignation was quite magnificent. And yet I don't suppose that ten per cent of the lower orders live correctly."

"I don't agree with a single word that you have said, and, what is more, Harry, I don't believe you do either."

Lord Henry stroked his pointed brown beard, and tapped the toe of his patent-leather boots with a tasselled malacca cane. "How English you are, Basil! If one puts forward an idea to a real Englishman - always a rash thing to do - he never dreams of considering whether an idea is right or wrong. The only thing he considers of any importance is whether one believes it one's self. Now, the value of an idea has nothing whatsoever to do with the sincerity of the man who expresses it. Indeed, the probabilities are that the more insincere the man is, the more purely intellectual will the idea be, as in that case it will not be coloured by either his wants, his desires, or his prejudices. However, I don't propose to discuss politics, sociology, or metaphysics with you. I like persons better than principles. Tell me more about Dorian Gray. How often do you see him?"

"Every day. I couldn't be happy if I didn't see him every day. Of course sometimes it is only for a few minutes. But a few minutes with somebody one worships means a great deal."

"But you don't really worship him?"

"I do."

"How extraordinary! I thought you would never care for anything but your painting – your art, I should say. Art sounds better, doesn't it?"

"He is all my art to me now. I sometimes think, Harry, that there are only two eras of any importance in the history of the world. The first is the appearance of a new medium for art, and the second is the appearance of a new personality for art also. What the invention of oil-painting was to the Venetians, the face of Antinous was to late Greek sculpture, and the face of Dorian Gray will some day be to me. It is not merely that I paint from him, draw from him, model from him. Of course I have done all that. He has stood as Paris in dainty armour, and as Adonis with huntsman's cloak and polished boar-spear. Crowned with heavy lotus-blossoms, he has sat on the prow of Adrian's barge, looking into the green, turbid Nile. He has leaned over the still pool of some Greek woodland, and seen in the water's silent silver the wonder of his own beauty. But he is much more to me than that. I won't tell you that I am dissatisfied with what I have done of him, or that his beauty is such that art cannot express it. There is nothing that art cannot express, and I know that the work I have done since I met Dorian Gray is good work, is the best work of my life. But in some curious way – I wonder will you understand me? – his personality has suggested to me an entirely new manner in art, an entirely new mode of style. I see things differently, I think of them differently. I can now re-create life in a way that was hidden from me before. 'A dream of form in days of thought' – who is it who says that? I forget; but it is what Dorian

Gray has been to me. The mere visible presence of this lad - for he seems to me little more than a lad, though he is really over twenty - his mere visible presence - ah! I wonder can you realise all that that means? Unconsciously he defines for me the lines of a fresh school, a school that is to have in itself all the passion of the romantic spirit, all the perfection of the spirit that is Greek. The harmony of soul and body - how much that is! We in our madness have separated the two, and have invented a realism that is bestial, an ideality that is void. Harry! Harry! if you only knew what Dorian Gray is to me! You remember that landscape of mine, for which Agnew offered me such a huge price, but which I would not part with? It is one of the best things I have ever done. And why is it so? Because, while I was painting it, Dorian Gray sat beside me."

"Basil, this is quite wonderful! I must see Dorian Gray."

Hallward got up from the seat, and walked up and down the garden. After some time he came back.

"You don't understand, Harry," he said. "Dorian Gray is merely to me a motive in art. He is never more present in my work than when no image of him is there. He is simply a suggestion, as I have said, of a new manner. I see him in the curves of certain lines, in the loveliness and the subtleties of certain colours. That is all."

"Then why won't you exhibit his portrait?"

"Because I have put into it all the extraordinary romance of which, of course, I have never dared to speak to him. He knows nothing about it. He will never know anything about it. But the world might guess it; and I will not bare my soul to their shallow, prying eyes. My heart shall never be put under their microscope. There is too much of myself in the thing, Harry - too much of myself!"

"Poets are not so scrupulous as you are. They know how useful passion is for publication. Nowadays a broken heart will run to many editions."

"I hate them for it. An artist should create beautiful things, but should put nothing of his own life into them. We live in an age when men treat art as if it were meant to be a form of autobiography. We have lost the abstract sense of beauty. If I live, I will show the world what it is; and for that reason the world shall never see my portrait of Dorian Gray."

"I think you are wrong, Basil, but I won't argue with you. It is only the intellectually lost who ever argue. Tell me, is Dorian Gray very fond of you?"

Hallward considered for a few moments. "He likes me," he answered after a pause; "I know he likes me. Of course I flatter him dreadfully. I find strange pleasure in saying things to him that I know I shall be sorry for having said. I give myself away. As a rule, he is charming to me, and we walk home together from the club arm in arm, or sit in the studio and talk of a thousand things. Now and then, however, he is horribly thoughtless, and seems to take a real delight in giving me pain. Then I feel, Harry, that I have given away my whole soul to some one who treats it as if it were a flower to put in his coat, a bit of decoration to charm his vanity, an ornament for a summer's day."

"Days in summer, Basil, are apt to linger. Perhaps you will tire sooner than he will. It is a sad thing to think of, but there is no doubt that Genius lasts longer than Beauty. That accounts for the fact that we all take such pains to over-educate ourselves. In the wild struggle for existence, we want to have something that endures, and so we fill our minds with rubbish and facts in the silly hope of keeping our place. The thoroughly well informed man – that is the modern ideal. And the mind of the thoroughly well informed man is a dreadful thing. It is like a bric-a-brac shop, all monsters and dust, and everything priced above its proper value. I think you will tire first, all the same. Some day you will look at Gray, and he will seem to you to be a little out of drawing, or you won't like his tone of colour, or something. You will bitterly reproach him in your own heart, and seriously think that he has behaved very badly to you. The next time he calls, you will be perfectly cold and indifferent. It will be a great pity, for it will alter you. The worst of having a romance is that it leaves one so unromantic."

"Harry don't talk like that. As long as I live, the personality of Dorian Gray will dominate me. You can't feel what I feel. You change too often."

"Ah, my dear Basil, that is exactly why I can feel it. Those who are faithful know only the pleasures of love: it is the faithless who know love's tragedies."

And Lord Henry struck a light on a dainty silver case, and began to smoke a cigarette with a self-conscious and self-satisfied air, as if he had summoned up life in a phrase. There was a rustle of chirruping sparrows in the ivy, and the blue cloud-shadows chased themselves across the grass like swallows. How pleasant it was in the garden! And how delightful other people's emotions were! – much more delightful than their ideas, it seemed to him. One's own soul, and the passions of one's friends – those were the fascinating things in life. He thought with pleasure of the tedious luncheon that he had missed by staying so long with Basil Hallward. Had he gone to his aunt's, he would have been sure to meet Lord Goodbody there, and the whole conversation would have been about the housing of the poor, and the necessity for model lodging-houses. It was charming to have escaped all that! As he thought of his aunt, an idea seemed to strike him. He turned to Hallward, and said, "My dear fellow, I have just remembered."

"Remembered what, Harry?"

"Where I heard the name of Dorian Gray."

"Where was it?" asked Hallward, with a slight frown.

"Don't look so angry, Basil. It was at my aunt's, Lady Agatha's. She told me she had discovered a wonderful young man, who was going to help her in the East End, and that his name was Dorian Gray. I am bound to state that she never told me he was good-looking. Women have no appreciation of good looks. At least, good women have not. She said that he was very earnest, and had a beautiful nature. I at once pictured to myself a creature with spectacles and lank hair, horridly freckled, and tramping about on huge feet. I wish I had known it was your friend."

"I am very glad you didn't, Harry."

"Why?"

"I don't want you to meet him."

"Mr. Dorian Gray is in the studio, sir," said the butler, coming into the garden.

"You must introduce me now," cried Lord Henry, laughing.

Basil Hallward turned to the servant, who stood blinking in the sunlight. "Ask Mr. Gray to wait, Parker: I will be in a few moments." The man bowed, and went up the walk.

Then he looked at Lord Henry. "Dorian Gray is my dearest friend," he said. "He has a simple and a beautiful nature. Your aunt was quite right in what she said of him. Don't spoil him for me. Don't try to influence him. Your influence would be bad. The world is wide, and has many marvellous people in it. Don't take away from me the one person that makes life absolutely lovely to me, and that gives to my art whatever wonder or charm it possesses. Mind, Harry, I trust you." He spoke very slowly, and the words seemed wrung out of him almost against his will.

"What nonsense you talk!" said Lord Henry, smiling, and, taking Hallward by the arm, he almost led him into the house.

TWO

As they entered they saw Dorian Gray. He was seated at the piano, with his back to them, turning over the pages of a volume of 'Schumann's Forest Scenes'. "You must lend me these, Basil," he cried. "I want to learn them. They are perfectly charming."

"That entirely depends on how you sit to-day, Dorian."

"Oh, I am tired of sitting, and I don't want a life-sized portrait of myself," answered the lad, swinging round on the music-stool, in a wilful, petulant manner. When he caught sight of Lord Henry, a faint blush coloured his cheeks for a moment, and he started up. "I beg your pardon, Basil, but I didn't know you had anyone with you."

"This is Lord Henry Wotton, Dorian, an old Oxford friend of mine. I have just been telling him what a capital sitter you were, and now you have spoiled everything."

"You have not spoiled my pleasure in meeting you, Mr. Gray," said Lord Henry, stepping forward and shaking him by the hand. "My aunt has often spoken to me about you. You are one of her favourites, and, I am afraid, one of her victims also."

"I am in Lady Agatha's black books at present," answered Dorian, with a funny look of penitence. "I promised to go to her club in Whitechapel with her last Tuesday, and I really forgot all about it.

We were to have played a duet together – three duets, I believe. I don't know what she will say to me. I am far too frightened to call."

"Oh, I will make your peace with my aunt. She is quite devoted to you. And I don't think it really matters about your not being there. The audience probably thought it was a duet. When Aunt Agatha sits down to the piano she makes quite enough noise for two people."

"That is very horrid to her, and not very nice to me," answered Dorian, laughing.

Lord Henry looked at him. Yes, he was certainly wonderfully handsome, with his finely-curved scarlet lips, his frank blue eyes, his crisp gold hair. There was something in his face that made one trust him at once. All the candour of youth was there, as well as all youth's passionate purity. One felt that he had kept himself unspotted from the world. No wonder Basil Hallward worshipped him. He was made to be worshipped.

"You are too charming to go in for philanthropy, Mr. Gray – far too charming." And Lord Henry flung himself down on the divan, and opened his cigarette-case.

Hallward had been busy mixing his colours and getting his brushes ready. He was looking worried and when he heard Lord Henry's last remark he glanced at him, hesitated for a moment, and then said, "Harry, I want to finish this picture to-day. Would you think it awfully rude of me if I asked you to go away?"

Lord Henry smiled, and looked at Dorian Gray. "Am I to go, Mr. Gray?" he asked.

"Oh, please don't, Lord Henry. I see that Basil is in one of his sulky moods; and I can't bear him when he sulks. Besides, I want you to tell me why I should not go in for philanthropy."

"I don't know that I shall tell you that, Mr. Gray. But I certainly will not run away now that you have asked me to stop. You don't really mind, Basil, do you? You have often told me that you liked your sitters to have some one to chat to."

Hallward bit his lip. "If Dorian wishes it, of co
stay. Dorian's whims are laws to everybody, except I

Lord Henry took up his hat and gloves
pressing, Basil, but I am afraid I must go. I have prom...
man at the Orleans. —Good-bye, Mr. Gray. Come and see me som...
afternoon in Curzon Street. I am nearly always at home at five
o'clock. Write to me when you are coming. I should be sorry to miss
you."

"Basil," cried Dorian Gray, "if Lord Henry goes I shall go too.
You never open your lips while you are painting, and it is horribly
dull standing on a platform and trying to look pleasant. Ask him to
stay. I insist upon it."

"Stay, Harry, to oblige Dorian, and to oblige me," said
Hallward, gazing intently at his picture. "It is quite true, I never talk
when I am working, and never listen either, and it must be
dreadfully tedious for my unfortunate sitters. I beg you to stay."

"But what about my man at the Orleans?"

Hallward laughed. "I don't think there will be any difficulty
about that. Sit down again, Harry. —And now, Dorian, get up on the
platform, and don't move about too much, or pay any attention to
what Lord Henry says. He has a very bad influence over all his
friends, with the exception of myself."

Dorian stepped up on the dais, with the air of a young
Greek martyr, and made a little moue of discontent to Lord Henry,
to whom he had rather taken a fancy. He was so unlike Hallward.
They made a delightful contrast. And he had such a beautiful voice.
After a few moments he said to him, "Have you really a very bad
influence, Lord Henry? As bad as Basil says?"

"There is no such thing as a good influence, Mr. Gray. All
influence is immoral – immoral from the scientific point of view."

"Why?"

"Because to influence a person is to give him one's own
soul. He does not think his natural thoughts, or burn with his natural

ions. His virtues are not real to him. His sins, if there are such things as sins, are borrowed. He becomes an echo of some one else's music, an actor of a part that has not been written for him. The aim of life is self-development. To realise one's nature perfectly – that is what each of us is here for. People are afraid of themselves, nowadays. They have forgotten the highest of all duties, the duty that one owes to one's self. Of course they are charitable. They feed the hungry, and clothe the beggar. But their own souls starve, and are naked. Courage has gone out of our race. Perhaps we never really had it. The terror of society, which is the basis of morals, the terror of God, which is the secret of religion – these are the two things that govern us. And yet—"

"Just turn your head a little more to the right, Dorian, like a good boy," said Hallward, deep in his work, and conscious only that a look had come into the lad's face that he had never seen there before.

"And yet," continued Lord Henry, in his low musical voice, and with that graceful wave of the hand that was always so characteristic of him, and that he had even in his Eton days, "I believe that if one man were to live his life out fully and completely, were to give form to every feeling, expression to every thought, reality to every dream – I believe that the world would gain such a fresh impulse of joy that we would forget all the maladies of mediaevalism, and return to the Hellenic ideal – to something finer, richer, than the Hellenic ideal, it may be. But the bravest man among us is afraid of himself. The mutilation of the savage has its tragic survival in the self-denial that mars our lives. We are punished for our refusals. Every impulse that we strive to strangle broods in the mind, and poisons us. The body sins once, and has done with its sin, for action is a mode of purification. Nothing remains then but the recollection of pleasure, or the luxury of a regret. The only way to get rid of a temptation is to yield to it. Resist it, and your soul grows sick with longing for the things it has forbidden to itself, with desire for what its monstrous laws have made monstrous and unlawful. It has been said that the great events of the world take place in the brain. It is in the brain, and the brain only, that the great sins of the world take place also. You, Mr. Gray, you yourself, with your rose-red youth and your rose-white boyhood, you have had passions that have made you afraid, thoughts that have filled you with terror, day-dreams and sleeping dreams whose mere memory might stain your cheek with shame—"

"Stop!" murmured Dorian Gray, "stop! you bewilder me. I don't know what to say. There is some answer to you, but I cannot find it. Don't speak. Let me think, or, rather, let me try not to think."

For nearly ten minutes he stood there motionless, with parted lips, and eyes strangely bright. He was dimly conscious that entirely fresh impulses were at work within him, and they seemed to him to have come really from himself. The few words that Basil's friend had said to him – words spoken by chance, no doubt, and with wilful paradox in them – had yet touched some secret chord, that had never been touched before, but that he felt was now vibrating and throbbing to curious pulses.

Music had stirred him like that. Music had troubled him many times. But music was not articulate. It was not a new world, but rather a new chaos, that it created in us. Words! Mere words! How terrible they were! How clear, and vivid, and cruel! One could not escape from them. And yet what a subtle magic there was in them! They seemed to be able to give a plastic form to formless things, and to have a music of their own as sweet as that of viol or of lute. Mere words! Was there anything so real as words?

Yes; there had been things in his boyhood that he had not understood. He understood them now. It seemed to him that he had been walking in fire. Why had he not known it?

Lord Henry watched him, with his sad smile. He knew the precise psychological moment when to say nothing. He felt intensely interested. He was amazed at the sudden impression that his words had produced, and, remembering a book that he had read when he was sixteen, which had revealed to him much that he had not known before, he wondered whether Dorian Gray was passing through the same experience. He had merely shot an arrow into the air. Had it hit the mark? How fascinating the lad was!

Hallward painted away with that marvellous bold touch of his, that had the true refinement and perfect delicacy that come only from strength. He was unconscious of the silence.

"Basil, I am tired of standing," cried Dorian Gray suddenly. "I must go out and sit in the garden. The air is stifling here."

"My dear fellow, I am so sorry. When I am painting, I can't think of anything else. But you never sat better. You were perfectly still. And I have caught the effect I wanted – the half-parted lips, and the bright look in the eyes. I don't know what Harry has been saying to you, but he has certainly made you have the most wonderful expression. I suppose he has been paying you compliments. You mustn't believe a word that he says."

"He has certainly not been paying me compliments. Perhaps that is the reason I don't think I believe anything he has told me."

"You know you believe it all," said Lord Henry, looking at him with his dreamy, heavy-lidded eyes. "I will go out to the garden with you. It is horridly hot in the studio. —Basil, let us have something iced to drink, something with strawberries in it."

"Certainly, Harry. Just touch the bell, and when Parker comes I will tell him what you want. I have got to work up this background, so I will join you later on. Don't keep Dorian too long. I have never been in better form for painting than I am to-day. This is going to be my masterpiece. It is my masterpiece as it stands."

Lord Henry went out to the garden, and found Dorian Gray burying his face in the great cool lilac-blossoms, feverishly drinking in their perfume as if it had been wine. He came close to him, and put his hand upon his shoulder. "You are quite right to do that," he murmured. "Nothing can cure the soul but the senses, just as nothing can cure the senses but the soul."

The lad started and drew back. He was bareheaded, and the leaves had tossed his rebellious curls and tangled all their gilded threads. There was a look of fear in his eyes, such as people have when they are suddenly awakened. His finely-chiselled nostrils quivered, and some hidden nerve shook the scarlet of his lips and left them trembling.

"Yes," continued Lord Henry, "that is one of the great senses of life – to cure the soul by means of the senses, and the senses by means of the soul. You are a wonderful creature. You know more than you think you know, just as you know less than you want to know."

Dorian Gray frowned and turned his head away. He could not help liking the tall, graceful young man who was standing by him. His romantic olive-coloured face and worn expression interested him. There was something in his low, languid voice that was absolutely fascinating. His cool, white, flower-like hands, even, had a curious charm. They moved, as he spoke, like music, and seemed to have a language of their own. But he felt afraid of him, and ashamed of being afraid. Why had it been left for a stranger to reveal him to himself? He had known Basil Hallward for months, but the friendship between them had never altered him. Suddenly there had come some one across his life who seemed to have disclosed to him life's mystery. And, yet, what was there to be afraid of? He was not a school-boy, or a girl. It was absurd to be frightened.

"Let us go and sit in the shade," said Lord Henry. "Parker has brought out the drinks, and if you stay any longer in this glare you will be quite spoiled, and Basil will never paint you again. You really must not let yourself become sunburnt. It would be very unbecoming to you."

"What does it matter?" cried Dorian, laughing, as he sat down on the seat at the end of the garden.

"It should matter everything to you, Mr. Gray."

"Why?"

"Because you have now the most marvellous youth, and youth is the one thing worth having."

"I don't feel that, Lord Henry."

"No, you don't feel it now. Some day, when you are old and wrinkled and ugly, when thought has seared your forehead with its lines, and passion branded your lips with its hideous fires, you will feel it, you will feel it terribly. Now, wherever you go, you charm the world. Will it always be so?

"You have a wonderfully beautiful face, Mr. Gray. Don't frown. You have. And Beauty is a form of Genius – is higher, indeed, than Genius, as it needs no explanation. It is one of the great facts of the world, like sunlight, or spring-time, or the reflection in dark waters of that silver shell we call the moon. It cannot be questioned. It has its divine right of sovereignty. It makes princes of those who have it. You smile? Ah! when you have lost it you won't smile.

"People say sometimes that Beauty is only superficial. That may be so. But at least it is not so superficial as Thought. To me, Beauty is the wonder of wonders. It is only shallow people who do not judge by appearances. The true mystery of the world is the visible, not the invisible.

"Yes, Mr. Gray, the gods have been good to you.

But what the gods give they quickly take away. You have only a few years in which really to live. When your youth goes, your beauty will go with it, and then you will suddenly discover that there are no triumphs left for you, or have to content yourself with those mean triumphs that the memory of your past will make more bitter than defeats. Every month as it wanes brings you nearer to something dreadful. Time is jealous of you, and wars against your lilies and your roses. You will become sallow, and hollow-cheeked, and dull-eyed. You will suffer horribly.

"Realise your youth while you have it. Don't squander the

gold of your days, listening to the tedious, trying to improve the hopeless failure, or giving away your life to the ignorant, the common, and the vulgar, which are the aims, the false ideals of our age. Live! Live the wonderful life that is in you! Let nothing be lost upon you. Be always searching for new sensations. Be afraid of nothing.

"A new hedonism – that is what our century wants. You might be its visible symbol. With your personality there is nothing you could not do. The world belongs to you for a season.

"The moment I met you I saw that you were quite unconscious of what you really are, what you really might be. There was so much about you that charmed me that I felt I must tell you something about yourself. I thought how tragic it would be if you were wasted. For there is such a little time that your youth will last – such a little time.

"The common hill-flowers wither, but they blossom again. The laburnum will be as golden next June as it is now. In a month there will be purple stars on the clematis, and year after year the green night of its leaves will have its purple stars. But we never get back our youth. The pulse of joy that beats in us at twenty, becomes sluggish. Our limbs fail, our senses rot. We degenerate into hideous puppets, haunted by the memory of the passions of which we were too much afraid, and the exquisite temptations that we did not dare to yield to. Youth! Youth!"

Dorian Gray listened, open-eyed and wondering. The spray of lilac fell from his hand upon the gravel. A furry bee came and buzzed round it for a moment. Then it began to scramble all over the fretted purple of the tiny blossoms. He watched it with that strange interest in trivial things that we try to develop when things of high import make us afraid, or when we are stirred by some new emotion, for which we cannot find expression, or when some thought that terrifies us lays sudden siege to the brain and calls on us to yield. After a time it flew away. He saw it creeping into the stained trumpet of a Tyrian convolvulus. The flower seemed to quiver, and then swayed gently to and fro.

Suddenly Hallward appeared at the door of the studio, and made frantic signs for them to come in. They turned to each other, and smiled.

"I am waiting," cried Hallward. "Do come in. The light is quite perfect, and you can bring your drinks."

They rose up, and sauntered down the walk together. Two green-and-white butterflies fluttered past them, and in the pear-tree at the end of the garden a thrush began to sing.

"You are glad you have met me, Mr. Gray," said Lord Henry, looking at him.

"Yes, I am glad now. I wonder shall I always be glad?"

"Always! That is a dreadful word. It makes me shudder when I hear it. Women are so fond of using it. They spoil every romance by trying to make it last forever. It is a meaningless word, too. The only difference between a caprice and a life-long passion is that the caprice lasts a little longer."

As they entered the studio, Dorian Gray put his hand upon Lord Henry's arm. "In that case, let our friendship be a caprice," he murmured, flushing at his own boldness, then stepped upon the platform and resumed his pose.

Lord Henry flung himself into a large wicker armchair, and watched him. The sweep and dash of the brush on the canvas made the only sound that broke the stillness, except when Hallward stepped back now and then to look at his work from a distance. In the slanting beams that streamed through the open doorway the dust danced and was golden. The heavy scent of the roses seemed to brood over everything.

After about a quarter of an hour, Hallward stopped painting, looked for a long time at Dorian Gray, and then for a long time at the picture, biting the end of one of his huge brushes, and smiling. "It is quite finished," he cried, at last, and stooping down he wrote his name in thin vermilion letters on the lefthand corner of the canvas.

Lord Henry came over and examined the picture. It was certainly a wonderful work of art, and a wonderful likeness as well.

"My dear fellow, I congratulate you most warmly," he said. "—Mr. Gray, come and look at yourself."

The lad started, as if awakened from some dream. "Is it really finished?" he murmured, stepping down from the platform.

"Quite finished," said Hallward. "And you have sat splendidly to-day. I am awfully obliged to you."

"That is entirely due to me," broke in Lord Henry. "Isn't it, Mr. Gray?"

Dorian made no answer, but passed listlessly in front of his picture and turned towards it. When he saw it he drew back, and his cheeks flushed for a moment with pleasure. A look of joy came into his eyes, as if he had recognized himself for the first time. He stood there motionless, and in wonder, dimly conscious that Hallward was speaking to him, but not catching the meaning of his words. The sense of his own beauty came on him like a revelation. He had never felt it before. Basil Hallward's compliments had seemed to him to be merely the charming exaggerations of friendship. He had listened to them, laughed at them, forgotten them. They had not influenced his nature. Then had come Lord Henry, with his strange panegyric on youth, his terrible warning of its brevity. That had stirred him at the time, and now, as he stood gazing at the shadow of his own loveliness, the full reality of the description flashed across him. Yes, there would be a day when his face would be wrinkled and wizen, his eyes dim and colourless, the grace of his figure broken and deformed. The scarlet would pass away from his lips, and the gold steal from his hair. The life that was to make his soul would mar his body. He would become ignoble, hideous, and uncouth.

As he thought of it, a sharp pang of pain struck like a knife across him, and made each delicate fibre of his nature quiver. His eyes deepened into amethyst, and a mist of tears came across them. He felt as if a hand of ice had been laid upon his heart.

"Don't you like it?" cried Hallward at last, stung a little by the lad's silence, and not understanding what it meant.

"Of course he likes it," said Lord Henry. "Who wouldn't like it? It is one of the greatest things in modern art. I will give you anything you like to ask for it. I must have it."

"It is not my property, Harry."

"Whose property is it?"

"Dorian's, of course."

"He is a very lucky fellow."

"How sad it is!" murmured Dorian Gray, with his eyes still fixed upon his own portrait. "How sad it is! I shall grow old, and horrid, and dreadful. But this picture will remain always young. It will never be older than this particular day in June... If it was only the other way! If it was I who were to be always young, and the picture that were to grow old! For this – for this – I would give everything! Yes, there is nothing in the whole world I would not give!"

"You would hardly care for that arrangement, Basil," cried Lord Henry, laughing. "It would be rather hard lines on you."

"I should object very strongly, Harry."

Dorian Gray turned and looked at him. "I believe you would, Basil. You like your art better than your friends. I am no more to you than a green bronze figure. Hardly as much, I dare say."

Hallward stared in amazement. It was so unlike Dorian to speak like that. What had happened? He seemed almost angry. His face was flushed and his cheeks burning.

"Yes," he continued, "I am less to you than your ivory Hermes or your silver Faun. You will like them always. How long will you like me? Till I have my first wrinkle, I suppose. I know, now, that when one loses one's good looks, whatever they may be, one loses everything. Your picture has taught me that. Lord Henry is perfectly right. Youth is the only thing worth having. When I find that I am growing old, I will kill myself."

Hallward turned pale, and caught his hand. "Dorian! Dorian!" he cried, "don't talk like that. I have never had such a friend as you, and I shall never have such another. You are not jealous of material things, are you?"

"I am jealous of everything whose beauty does not die. I am jealous of the portrait you have painted of me. Why should it keep what I must lose? Every moment that passes takes something from me, and gives something to it. Oh, if it was only the other way! If the picture could change, and I could be always what I am now! Why did you paint it? It will mock me some day – mock me horribly!" The hot tears welled into his eyes; he tore his hand away, and, flinging himself on the divan, he buried his face in the cushions, as if he was praying.

"This is your doing, Harry," said Hallward, bitterly.

"My doing?"

"Yes, yours, and you know it."

Lord Henry shrugged his shoulders. "It is the real Dorian Gray – that is all," he answered.

"It is now."

"If it is not, what have I got to do with it?"

"You should have gone away when I asked you."

"I stayed when you asked me."

"Harry, I can't quarrel with my two best friends at once, but between you both you have made me hate the finest piece of work I have ever done, and I will destroy it. What is it but canvas and colour? I will not let it come across our three lives and mar them."

Dorian Gray lifted his golden head from the pillow, and looked at him with pallid face and tear-stained eyes, as he walked over to the deal painting-table that was set beneath the large curtained window. What was he doing there? His fingers were straying about among the litter of tin tubes and dry brushes, seeking for something. Yes, it was the long palette-knife, with its thin blade of lithe steel. He had found it at last. He was going to rip up the canvas.

With a stifled sob he leaped from the couch, and rushing over to Hallward, tore the knife out of his hands, and flung it to the end of the studio. "Don't Basil, don't!" he cried. "It would be murder!"

"I am glad you appreciate my work at last, Dorian," said Hallward, coldly, when he had recovered from his surprise. "I never thought you would."

"Appreciate it? I am in love with it, Basil. It is part of myself, I feel that."

"Well, as soon as you are dry, you shall be varnished, and framed, and sent home. Then you can do what you like with yourself." And he walked across the room and rang the bell for tea. "You will have tea, of course, Dorian? And so will you, Harry? Tea is the only simple pleasure left to us."

"I don't like simple pleasures," said Lord Henry. "And I don't like scenes, except on the stage. What absurd fellows you are, both of you! I wonder who it was defined man as a rational animal. It was the most premature definition ever given. Man is many things, but he is not rational. I am glad he is not, after all: though I wish you chaps would not squabble over the picture. You had much better let me have it, Basil. This silly boy doesn't really want it, and I do."

"If you let any one have it but me, Basil, I will never forgive you!" cried Dorian Gray. "And I don't allow people to call me a silly boy."

"You know the picture is yours, Dorian. I gave it to you before it existed."

"And you know you have been a little silly, Mr. Gray, and that you don't really mind being called a boy."

"I should have minded very much this morning, Lord Henry."

"Ah! this morning! You have lived since then."

There came a knock at the door, and the butler entered with the tea-tray and set it down upon a small Japanese table. There was a rattle of cups and saucers and the hissing of a fluted Georgian urn. Two globe-shaped china dishes were brought in by a page. Dorian Gray went over and poured the tea out. The two men sauntered languidly to the table, and examined what was under the covers.

"Let us go to the theatre to-night," said Lord Henry. "There is sure to be something on, somewhere. I have promised to dine at White's, but it is only with an old friend, so I can send him a wire and say that I am ill, or that I am prevented from coming in consequence of a subsequent engagement. I think that would be a rather nice excuse: it would have the surprise of candour."

"It is such a bore putting on one's dress-clothes," muttered Hallward. "And, when one has them on, they are so horrid."

"Yes," answered Lord Henry, dreamily, "the costume of our day is detestable. It is so sombre, so depressing. Sin is the only colour-element left in modern life."

"You really must not say things like that before Dorian, Harry."

"Before which Dorian? The one who is pouring out tea for us, or the one in the picture?"

"Before either."

"I should like to come to the theatre with you, Lord Henry," said the lad.

"Then you shall come; and you will come too, Basil, won't you?"

"I can't really. I would sooner not. I have a lot of work to do."

"Well, then, you and I will go alone, Mr. Gray."

"I should like that awfully."

Basil Hallward bit his lip and walked over, cup in hand, to

the picture. "I will stay with the real Dorian," he said, sadly.

"Is it the real Dorian?" cried the original of the portrait, running across to him. "Am I really like that?"

"Yes; you are just like that."

"How wonderful, Basil!"

"At least you are like it in appearance. But it will never alter," said Hallward. "That is something."

"What a fuss people make about fidelity!" murmured Lord Henry. "And, after all, it is purely a question of physiology. It has nothing to do with our own will. It is either an unfortunate accident, or an unpleasant result of temperament. Young men want to be faithful, and are not; old men want to be faithless, and cannot: that is all one can say."

"Don't go to the theatre to-night, Dorian," said Hallward. "Stop and dine with me."

"I can't, really."

"Why?"

"Because I have promised Lord Henry to go with him."

"He won't like you better for keeping your promises. He always breaks his own. I beg you not to go."

Dorian Gray laughed and shook his head.

"I entreat you."

The lad hesitated, and looked over at Lord Henry, who was watching them from the tea-table with an amused smile.

"I must go, Basil," he answered.

"Very well," said Hallward; and he walked over and laid his cup down on the tray. "It is rather late, and, as you have to dress, you had better lose no time. Good-bye, Harry; good-bye, Dorian. Come and see me soon. Come to-morrow."

"Certainly."

"You won't forget?"

"No, of course not."

"And... Harry!"

"Yes, Basil?"

"Remember what I asked you, when in the garden this morning."

"I have forgotten it."

"I trust you."

"I wish I could trust myself," said Lord Henry, laughing. "— Come, Mr. Gray, my hansom is outside, and I can drop you at your own place. —Good-bye, Basil. It has been a most interesting afternoon."

As the door closed behind them, Hallward flung himself down on a sofa, and a look of pain came into his face.

THREE

One afternoon, a month later, Dorian Gray was reclining in a luxurious arm-chair in the little library of Lord Henry's house in Curzon Street. It was, in its way, a very charming room, with its high panelled wainscoting of olive-stained oak, its cream- coloured frieze and ceiling of raised plaster-work, and its brick-dust felt carpet strewn with long-fringed silk Persian rugs. On a tiny satin-wood table stood a statuette by Clodion, and beside it lay a copy of 'Les Cent Nouvelles', bound for Margaret of Valois by Clovis Eve, and powdered with the gilt daisies that the queen had selected for her device. Some large blue china jars, filled with parrot-tulips, were ranged on the mantel-shelf, and through the small leaded panes of the window streamed the apricot-coloured light of a summer's day in London.

Lord Henry had not come in yet. He was always late on principle, his principle being that punctuality is the thief of time. So the lad was looking rather sulky, as with listless fingers he turned over the pages of an elaborately-illustrated edition of 'Manon Lescaut' that he had found in one of the bookcases. The formal monotonous ticking of the Louis Quatorze clock annoyed him. Once or twice he thought of going away.

At last he heard a light step outside, and the door opened.

"How late you are, Harry!" he murmured.

"I am afraid it is not Harry, Mr. Gray," said a woman's voice.

He glanced quickly round, and rose to his feet. "I beg your pardon. I thought—"

"You thought it was my husband. It is only his wife. You must let me introduce myself. I know you quite well by your photographs. I think my husband has got twenty-seven of them."

"Not twenty-seven, Lady Henry?"

"Well, twenty-six, then. And I saw you with him the other night at the Opera." She laughed nervously, as she spoke, and watched him with her vague forget-me-not eyes. She was a curious woman, whose dresses always looked as if they had been designed in a rage and put on in a tempest. She was always in love with somebody, and, as her passion was never returned, she had kept all her illusions. She tried to look picturesque, but only succeeded in being untidy. Her name was Victoria, and she had a perfect mania for going to church.

"That was at 'Lohengrin', Lady Henry, I think?"

"Yes, it was at dear 'Lohengrin'. I like Wagner's music better than any other music. It is so loud that one can talk the whole time, without people hearing what one says. That is a great advantage: don't you think so, Mr. Gray?"

The same nervous staccato laugh broke from her thin lips, and her fingers began to play with a long paper-knife.

Dorian smiled, and shook his head: "I am afraid I don't think so, Lady Henry. I never talk during music – at least during good music. If one hears bad music, it is one's duty to drown it out by conversation."

"Ah! that is one of Harry's views, isn't it, Mr. Gray? But you must not think I don't like good music. I adore it, but I am afraid of it. It makes me too romantic. I have simply worshipped pianists – two at a time, sometimes. I don't know what it is about them. Perhaps it is that they are foreigners. They all are, aren't they? Even those that are born in England become foreigners after a time, don't they? It is so clever of them, and such a compliment to art. Makes it quite cosmopolitan, doesn't it? You have never been to any of my parties, have you, Mr. Gray? You must come. I can't afford orchids, but I spare no expense in foreigners. They make one's rooms look so picturesque. But here is Harry! – Harry, I came in to look for you, to ask you something – I forget what it was – and I found Mr. Gray here. We have had such a pleasant chat about music. We have quite the same views. No; I think our views are quite different. But he has been most pleasant. I am glad I've seen him."

"I am charmed, my love, quite charmed," said Lord Henry, elevating his dark crescent-shaped eye-brows and looking at them both with an amused smile. – "So sorry I am late, Dorian. I went to look after a piece of old brocade in Wardour Street, and had to bargain for hours for it. Nowadays people know the price of everything, and the value of nothing."

"I am afraid I must be going," exclaimed Lady Henry, after an awkward silence, with her silly sudden laugh. "I have promised to drive with the duchess. – Good-bye, Mr. Gray. – Good-bye, Harry. You are dining out, I suppose? So am I. Perhaps I shall see you at Lady Thornbury's."

"I dare say, my dear," said Lord Henry, shutting the door behind her, as she flitted out of the room, looking like a bird-of-paradise that had been out in the rain, and leaving a faint odour of patchouli behind her. Then he shook hands with Dorian Gray, lit a cigarette, and flung himself down on the sofa.

"Never marry a woman with straw-coloured hair, Dorian," He said, after a few puffs.

"Why, Harry?"

"Because they are so sentimental."

"But I like sentimental people."

"Never marry at all, Dorian. Men marry because they are tired; women because they are curious: both are disappointed."

"I don't think I am likely to marry, Harry. I am too much in love. That is one of your aphorisms. I am putting it into practice, as I do everything you say."

"Whom are you in love with?" said Lord Henry, looking at him with a curious smile.

"With an actress," said Dorian Gray, blushing.

Lord Henry shrugged his shoulders. "That is a rather commonplace debut," he murmured.

"You would not say so if you saw her, Harry."

"Who is she?"

"Her name is Sibyl Vane."

"Never heard of her."

"No one has. People will some day, however. She is a genius."

"My dear boy, no woman is a genius: women are a decorative sex. They never have anything to say, but they say it charmingly. They represent the triumph of matter over mind, just as we men represent the triumph of mind over morals. There are only two kinds of women, the plain and the coloured. The plain women are very useful. If you want to gain a reputation for respectability, you have merely to take them down to supper. The other women are very charming. They commit one mistake, however. They paint in order to try to look young. Our grandmothers painted in order to try to talk brilliantly. 'Rouge' and 'esprit' used to go together. That has all gone out now. As long as a woman can look ten years younger than her own daughter, she is perfectly satisfied. As for conversation, there are only five women in London worth talking to and two of these can't be admitted into decent society. However, tell me about your genius. How long have you known her?"

"About three weeks. Not so much. About two weeks and two days."

"How did you come across her?"

"I will tell you, Harry; but you mustn't be unsympathetic

about it. After all, it never would have happened if I had not met you. You filled me with a wild desire to know everything about life. For days after I met you, something seemed to throb in my veins. As I lounged in the Park or strolled down Piccadilly, I used to look at every one who passed me and wonder with a mad curiosity what sort of lives they led. Some of them fascinated me. Others filled me with terror. There was an exquisite poison in the air. I had a passion for sensations.

"One evening about seven o'clock I determined to go out in search of some adventure. I felt that this grey, monstrous London of ours, with its myriads of people, its splendid sinners, and its sordid sins, as you once said, must have something in store for me. I fancied a thousand things.

"The mere danger gave me a sense of delight. I remembered what you had said to me on that wonderful night when we first dined together, about the search for beauty being the poisonous secret of life. I don't know what I expected, but I went out, and wandered eastward, soon losing my way in a labyrinth of grimy streets and black, grassless squares. About half-past eight I passed by a little third-rate theatre, with great flaring gas-jets and gaudy play-bills. A hideous Jew, in the most amazing waistcoat I ever beheld in my life, was standing at the entrance, smoking a vile cigar. He had greasy ringlets, and an enormous diamond blazed in the centre of a soiled shirt. ''Ave a box, my lord?' he said, when he saw me, and took off his hat with an act of gorgeous servility. There was something about him, Harry, that amused me. He was such a monster. You will laugh at me, I know, but I really went in and paid a whole guinea for the stage-box. To the present day I can't make out why I did so; and yet if I hadn't! – my dear Harry, if I hadn't, I would have missed the greatest romance of my life. I see you are laughing. It is horrid of you!"

"I am not laughing, Dorian; at least I am not laughing at you. But you should not say the greatest romance of your life. You should say the first romance of your life. You will always be loved, and you will always be in love with love. There are exquisite things in store for you. This is merely the beginning."

"Do you think my nature so shallow?" cried Dorian Gray, angrily.

"No; I think your nature so deep."

"How do you mean?"

"My dear boy, people who only love once in their lives are really the shallow people. What they call their loyalty, and their fidelity, I call either the lethargy of custom or the lack of imagination. Faithlessness is to the emotional life what consistency is to the intellectual life – simply a confession of failure. But I don't want to interrupt you. Go on with your story."

"Well, I found myself seated in a horrid little private box, with a vulgar drop-scene staring me in the face. I looked out behind the curtain, and surveyed the house. It was a tawdry affair, all Cupids and cornucopias, like a third-rate wedding-cake. The gallery and pit were fairly full, but the two rows of dingy stalls were quite empty, and there was hardly a person in what I suppose they call the dress-circle. Women went about with oranges and ginger-beer, and there was a terrible consumption of nuts going on."

"It must have been just like the palmy days of the British Drama."

"Just like, I should fancy, and very horrid. I began to wonder what on earth I should do, when I caught sight of the play-bill. What do you think the play was, Harry?"

"I should think 'The Idiot Boy, or Dumb but Innocent'. Our fathers used to like that sort of piece, I believe. The longer I live, Dorian, the more keenly I feel that whatever was good enough for our fathers is not good enough for us. In art, as in politics, 'les grand pères ont toujours tort'."

"This play was good enough for us, Harry. It was 'Romeo and Juliet'. I must admit I was rather annoyed at the idea of seeing

Shakespeare done in such a wretched hole of a place. Still, I felt interested, in a sort of way. At any rate, I determined to wait for the first act. There was a dreadful orchestra, presided over by a young Jew who sat at a cracked piano, that nearly drove me away, but at last the drop-scene was drawn up, and the play began. Romeo was a stout elderly gentleman, with corked eyebrows, a husky tragedy voice, and a figure like a beer-barrel. Mercutio was almost as bad. He was played by the low-comedian, who had introduced gags of his own and was on most familiar terms with the pit. They were as grotesque as the scenery, and that looked as if it had come out of a pantomime of fifty years ago. But Juliet! Harry, imagine a girl, hardly seventeen years of age, with a little flower-like face, a small Greek head with plaited coils of dark-brown hair, eyes that were violet wells of passion, lips that were like the petals of a rose. She was the loveliest thing I had ever seen in my life. You said to me once that pathos left you unmoved, but that beauty, mere beauty, could fill your eyes with tears. I tell you, Harry, I could hardly see this girl for the mist of tears that came across me. And her voice – I never heard such a voice. It was very low at first, with deep mellow notes, that seemed to fall singly upon one's ear. Then it became a little louder, and sounded like a flute or a distant hautbois. In the garden-scene it had all the tremulous ecstasy that one hears just before dawn when nightingales are singing. There were moments, later on, when it had the wild passion of violins. You know how a voice can stir one. Your voice and the voice of Sibyl Vane are two things that I shall never forget. When I close my eyes, I hear them, and each of them says something different. I don't know which to follow. Why should I not love her? Harry, I do love her. She is everything to me in life. Night after night I go to see her play. One evening she is Rosalind, and the next evening she is Imogen. I have seen her die in the gloom of an Italian tomb, sucking the poison from her lover's lips. I have watched her wandering through the forest of Arden, disguised as a pretty boy in hose and doublet and dainty cap. She has been mad, and has come into the presence of a guilty king, and given him rue to wear, and bitter herbs to taste of. She has been innocent, and the black hands of jealousy have crushed her reed-like throat. I have seen her in every age and in every costume. Ordinary women never appeal to one's imagination. They are limited to their century. No glamour ever transfigures them. One knows their minds as easily as one knows their bonnets. One can always find them. There is no mystery in one of them. They ride in the Park in the morning, and chatter at tea-parties in the afternoon. They have their stereotyped smile, and their fashionable manner. They are quite obvious. But an actress! How different an actress is! Why didn't you tell me that the only thing worth loving is an actress?"

"Because I have loved so many of them, Dorian."

"Oh, yes, horrid people with dyed hair and painted faces."

"Don't run down dyed hair and painted faces. There is an extraordinary charm in them, sometimes."

"I wish now I had not told you about Sibyl Vane."

"You could not have helped telling me, Dorian. All through your life you will tell me everything you do."

"Yes, Harry, I believe that is true. I cannot help telling you things. You have a curious influence over me. If I ever did a crime, I would come and confide it to you. You would understand me."

"People like you – the wilful sunbeams of life – don't commit crimes, Dorian. But I am much obliged for the compliment, all the same. And now tell me – reach me the matches, like a good boy: thanks – tell me, what are your relations with Sibyl Vane?"

Dorian Gray leaped to his feet, with flushed cheeks and burning eyes. "Harry, Sibyl Vane is sacred!"

"It is only the sacred things that are worth touching, Dorian," said Lord Henry, with a strange touch of pathos in his voice. "But why should you be annoyed? I suppose she will be yours some day. When one is in love, one always begins by deceiving one's self, and one always ends by deceiving others. That is what the world calls romance. You know her, at any rate, I suppose?"

"Of course I know her. On the first night I was at the theatre, the horrid Jew came round to the box after the performance was over, and offered to bring me behind the scenes and introduce me to her. I was furious with him, and told him that Juliet had been dead for hundreds of years, and that her body was lying in a marble tomb in Verona. I think, from his blank look of amazement, that he thought I had taken too much champagne, or something."

"I am not surprised."

"I was not surprised either. Then he asked me if I wrote for any of the newspapers. I told him I never even read them. He seemed terribly disappointed at that, and confided to me that all the dramatic critics were in a conspiracy against him, and that they were all to be bought."

"I believe he was quite right there. But, on the other hand, most of them are not at all expensive."

"Well, he seemed to think they were beyond his means. By this time the lights were being put out in the theatre, and I had to go. He wanted me to try some cigars which he strongly recommended. I declined. The next night, of course, I arrived at the theatre again. When he saw me he made me a low bow, and assured me that I was a patron of art. He was a most offensive brute, though he had an extraordinary passion for Shakespeare. He told me once, with an air of pride, that his three bankruptcies were entirely due to the poet, whom he insisted on calling 'The Bard'. He seemed to think it a distinction."

"It was a distinction, my dear Dorian – a great distinction. But when did you first speak to Miss Sibyl Vane?"

"The third night. She had been playing Rosalind. I could not help going round. I had thrown her some flowers, and she had looked at me; at least I fancied that she had. The old Jew was persistent. He seemed determined to bring me behind, so I consented. It was curious my not wanting to know her, wasn't it?"

"No; I don't think so."

"My dear Harry, why?"

"I will tell you some other time. Now I want to know about the girl."

"Sibyl? Oh, she was so shy, and so gentle. There is something of a child about her. Her eyes opened wide in exquisite wonder when I told her what I thought of her performance, and she seemed quite unconscious of her power. I think we were both rather nervous. The old Jew stood grinning at the doorway of the dusty greenroom, making elaborate speeches about us both, while we stood looking at each other like children. He would insist on calling me 'My Lord', so I had to assure Sibyl that I was not anything of the kind. She said quite simply to me, 'You look more like a prince.'"

"Upon my word, Dorian, Miss Sibyl knows how to pay compliments."

"You don't understand her, Harry. She regarded me merely as a person in a play. She knows nothing of life. She lives with her mother, a faded tired woman who played Lady Capulet in a sort of magenta dressing-wrapper on the first night, and who looks as if she had seen better days."

"I know that look. It always depresses me."

"The Jew wanted to tell me her history, but I said it did not interest me."

"You were quite right. There is always something infinitely mean about other people's tragedies."

"Sibyl is the only thing I care about. What is it to me where she came from? From her little head to her little feet, she is absolutely and entirely divine. I go to see her act every night of my life, and every night she is more marvellous."

"That is the reason, I suppose, that you will never dine with me now. I thought you must have some curious romance on hand. You have; but it is not quite what I expected."

"My dear Harry, we either lunch or sup together every day, and I have been to the Opera with you several times."

"You always come dreadfully late."

"Well, I can't help going to see Sibyl play, even if it is only for an act. I get hungry for her presence; and when I think of the wonderful soul that is hidden away in that little ivory body, I am filled with awe."

"You can dine with me to-night, Dorian, can't you?"

He shook his head. "To-night she is Imogen," he answered, "and to-morrow night she will be Juliet."

"When is she Sibyl Vane?"

"Never."

"I congratulate you."

"How horrid you are! She is all the great heroines of the world in one. She is more than an individual. You laugh, but I tell you she has genius. I love her, and I must make her love me. You, who know all the secrets of life, tell me how to charm Sibyl Vane to love me! I want to make Romeo jealous. I want the dead lovers of the world to hear our laughter, and grow sad. I want a breath of our passion to stir their dust into consciousness, to wake their ashes into pain. My God, Harry, how I worship her!" He was walking up and down the room as he spoke. Hectic spots of red burned on his cheeks. He was terribly excited.

Lord Henry watched him with a subtle sense of pleasure. How different he was now from the shy, frightened boy he had met in Basil Hallward's studio! His nature had developed like a flower, had borne blossoms of scarlet flame. Out of its secret hiding-place had crept his Soul, and Desire had come to meet it on the way.

"And what do you propose to do?" said Lord Henry, at last.

"I want you and Basil to come with me some night and see her act. I have not the slightest fear of the result. You won't be able to refuse to recognise her genius. Then we must get her out of the Jew's hands. She is bound to him for three years – at least for two years and eight months – from the present time. I will have to pay him something, of course. When all that is settled, I will take a West End theatre and bring her out properly. She will make the world as mad as she has made me."

"Impossible, my dear boy!"

"Yes, she will. She has not merely art, consummate art-instinct, in her, but she has personality also; and you have often told me that it is personalities, not principles, that move the age."

"Well, what night shall we go?"

"Let me see. To-day is Tuesday. Let us fix to-morrow. She plays Juliet to-morrow."

"All right. The Bristol at eight o'clock; and I will get Basil."

"Not eight, Harry, please. Half-past six. We must be there before the curtain rises. You must see her in the first act where she meets Romeo."

"Half-past six! What an hour! It will be like having a meat-tea. However, just as you wish. Shall you see Basil between this and then? Or shall I write to him?"

"Dear Basil! I have not laid eyes on him for a week. It is rather horrid of me, as he has sent me my portrait in the most wonderful frame designed by himself, and, though I am a little jealous of it for being a whole month younger than I am, I must admit that I delight in it. Perhaps you had better write to him. I don't want to see him alone. He says things that annoy me."

Lord Henry smiled. "He gives you good advice, I suppose. People are very fond of giving away what they need most themselves."

"You don't mean to say that Basil has got any passion or any romance in him?"

"I don't know whether he has any passion, but he certainly has romance," said Lord Henry, with an amused look in his eyes. "Has he never let you know that?"

"Never. I must ask him about it. I am rather surprised to

hear it. He is the best of fellows, but he seems to me to be just a bit of a Philistine. Since I have known you, Harry, I have discovered that."

"Basil, my dear boy, puts everything that is charming in him into his work. The consequence is that he has nothing left for life but his prejudices, his principles, and his common sense. The only artists I have ever known who are personally delightful are bad artists. Good artists give everything to their art, and consequently are perfectly uninteresting in themselves. A great poet, a really great poet, is the most unpoetical of all creatures. But inferior poets are absolutely fascinating. The worse their rhymes are, the more picturesque they look. The mere fact of having published a book of second-rate sonnets makes a man quite irresistible. He lives the poetry that he cannot write. The others write the poetry that they dare not realise."

"I wonder is that really so, Harry?" said Dorian Gray, putting some perfume on his handkerchief out of a large gold-topped bottle that stood on the table. "It must be, if you say so. And now I must be off. Imogen is waiting for me. Don't forget about to-morrow. Good-bye."

As he left the room, Lord Henry's heavy eyelids drooped, and he began to think. Certainly few people had ever interested him so much as Dorian Gray, and yet the lad's mad adoration of some one else caused him not the slightest pang of annoyance or jealousy. He was pleased by it. It made him a more interesting study. He had been always enthraled by the methods of science, but the ordinary subject-matter of science had seemed to him trivial and of no import. And so he had begun by vivisecting himself, as he had ended by vivisecting others. Human life – that appeared to him the one thing worth investigating. There was nothing else of any value, compared to it. It was true that as one watched life in its curious crucible of pain and pleasure, one could not wear over one's face a mask of glass, or keep the sulphurous fumes from troubling the brain and making the imagination turbid with monstrous fancies and misshapen dreams. There were poisons so subtle that to know their properties one had to sicken of them. There were maladies so strange that one had to pass through them if one sought to understand their nature. And, yet, what a great reward one received! How wonderful the whole world became to one! To note the curious hard logic of passion, and the emotional coloured life of the intellect – to observe where they met, and where they separated, at what point they became one, and at what point they were at discord – there was a delight in that! What matter what the cost was? One could never pay too high a price for any sensation.

He was conscious – and the thought brought a gleam of pleasure into his brown agate eyes – that it was through certain words of his, musical words said with musical utterance, that Dorian Gray's soul had turned to this white girl and bowed in worship before her. To a large extent, the lad was his own creation. He had made him premature. That was something. Ordinary people waited till life disclosed to them its secrets, but to the few, to the elect, the mysteries of life were revealed before the veil was drawn away. Sometimes this was the effect of art, and chiefly of the art of literature, which dealt immediately with the passions and the intellect. But now and then a complex personality took the place and assumed the office of art, was indeed, in its way, a real work of art, Life having its elaborate masterpieces, just as poetry has, or sculpture, or painting.

Yes, the lad was premature. He was gathering harvest while it was yet spring. The pulse and passion of youth were in him, but he was becoming self-conscious. It was delightful to watch him. With his beautiful face, and his beautiful soul, he was a thing to wonder at. It was no matter how it all ended, or was destined to end. He was like one of those gracious figures in a pageant or a play, whose joys seem to be remote from one, but whose sorrows stir one's sense of beauty, and whose wounds are like red roses.

Soul and body, body and soul – how mysterious they were! There was animalism in the soul, and the body had its moments of spirituality. The senses could refine, and the intellect could degrade. Who could say where the fleshly impulse ceased, or the psychical impulse began? How shallow were the arbitrary definitions of ordinary psychologists! And yet how difficult to decide between the claims of the various schools! Was the soul a shadow seated in the house of sin? Or was the body really in the soul, as Giordano Bruno thought? The separation of spirit from matter was a mystery, and the union of spirit with matter was a mystery also.

He began to wonder whether we should ever make psychology so absolute a science that each little spring of life would be revealed to us. As it was, we always misunderstood ourselves, and rarely understood others. Experience was of no ethical value. It was merely the name we gave to our mistakes. Men had, as a rule, regarded it as a mode of warning, had claimed for it a certain moral efficacy in the formation of character, had praised it as something that taught us what to follow and showed us what to avoid. But there was no motive power in experience. It was as little of an active cause as conscience itself. All that it really demonstrated was that our future would be the same as our past, and that the sin we had done once, and with loathing, we would do many times, and with joy.

It was clear to him that the experimental method was the only method by which one could arrive at any scientific analysis of the passions; and certainly Dorian Gray was a subject made to his hand, and seemed to promise rich and fruitful results. His sudden mad love for Sibyl Vane was a psychological phenomenon of no small interest. There was no doubt that curiosity had much to do with it, curiosity and the desire for new experiences; yet it was not a simple, but rather a very complex passion. What there was in it of the purely sensuous instinct of boyhood had been transformed by the workings of the imagination, changed into something that seemed to the boy himself to be remote from sense, and was for that very reason all the more dangerous. It was the passions about whose origin we deceived ourselves that tyrannised most strongly over us. Our weakest motives were those of whose nature we were conscious. It often happened that when we thought we were experimenting on others we were really experimenting on ourselves.

While Lord Henry sat dreaming on these things, a knock came to the door, and his valet entered, and reminded him it was time to dress for dinner. He got up and looked out into the street. The sunset had smitten into scarlet gold the upper windows of the house opposite. The panes glowed like plates of heated metal. The sky above was like a faded rose. He thought of Dorian Gray's young fiery-coloured life, and wondered how it was all going to end.

When he arrived home, about half-past twelve o'clock, he saw a telegram laying on the hall-table. He opened it and found it was from Dorian. It was to tell him that he was engaged to be married to Sibyl Vane.

FOUR

"I suppose you have heard the news Basil?" said Lord Henry on the following evening, as Hallward was shown into a little private room at the Bristol where dinner had been laid for three.

"No, Harry," answered Hallward, giving his hat and coat to the bowing waiter. "What is it? Nothing about politics, I hope?" They don't interest me. There is hardly a single person in the House of Commons worth painting; though many of them would be the better for a little whitewashing."

"Dorian Gray is engaged to be married," said Lord Henry, watching him as he spoke.

Hallward turned perfectly pale, and a curious look flashed for a moment into his eyes, and then passed away, leaving them dull. "Dorian engaged to be married!" he cried. "Impossible!"

"It is perfectly true."

"To whom?"

"To some little actress or other."

"I can't believe it. Dorian is far too sensible."

"Dorian is far too wise not to do foolish things now and then, my dear Basil."

"Marriage is hardly a thing one can do now and then, Harry," said Hallward, smiling.

"Except in America. But I didn't say he was married. I said he was engaged to be married. There is a great difference. I have a distinct remembrance of being married, but I have no recollection at all of being engaged. I am inclined to think that I never was engaged."

"But think of Dorian's birth, and position, and wealth. It would be absurd for him to marry so much beneath him."

"If you want him to marry this girl, tell him that, Basil. He is sure to do it then. Whenever a man does a thoroughly stupid thing, it is always from the noblest motives."

"I hope the girl is good, Harry. I don't want to see Dorian tied to some vile creature, who might degrade his nature and ruin his intellect."

"Oh, she is more than good – she is beautiful," murmured Lord Henry, sipping a glass of vermouth and orange-bitters. "Dorian says she is beautiful and he is not often wrong about things of that kind. Your portrait of him has quickened his appreciation of the personal appearance of other people. It has had that excellent effect, among others. We are to see her to-night, if that boy doesn't forget his appointment."

"But do you approve of it, Harry?" asked Hallward, walking up and down the room, and biting his lip. "You can't approve of it, really. It is some silly infatuation."

"I never approve, or disapprove, of anything now. It is an absurd attitude to take towards life. We are not sent into the world to air our moral prejudices. I never take any notice of what common people say, and I never interfere with what charming people do. If a personality fascinates me, whatever the personality chooses to do is absolutely delightful to me. Dorian Gray falls in love with a beautiful girl who acts Shakespeare, and proposes to marry her. Why not? If he wedded Messalina he would be none the less interesting. You know I am not a champion of marriage. The real drawback to marriage is that it makes one unselfish. And unselfish people are colourless. They lack individuality. Still, there are certain temperaments that marriage makes more complex. They retain their egotism, and add to it many other egos. They are forced to have more than one life. They become more highly organised. Besides, every experience is of value, and, whatever one may say against marriage, it is certainly an experience. I hope that Dorian Gray will make this girl his wife, passionately adore her for six months, and then suddenly become fascinated by some one else. He would be a wonderful study."

"You don't mean all that, Harry; you know you don't. If Dorian Gray's life were spoiled, no one would be sorrier than yourself. You are much better than you pretend to be."

Lord Henry laughed. "The reason we all like to think so well of others is that we are all afraid for ourselves. The basis of optimism is sheer terror. We think that we are generous because we credit our neighbour with those virtues that are likely to benefit ourselves. We praise the banker that we may overdraw our account, and find good qualities in the highwayman in the hope that he may spare our pockets. I mean everything that I have said. I have the greatest contempt for optimism. And as for a spoiled life, no life is spoiled but one whose growth is arrested. If you want to mar a nature, you have merely to reform it. But here is Dorian himself. He will tell you more than I can."

"My dear Harry, my dear Basil, you must both congratulate me!" said the boy, throwing off his evening cape with its satin-lined wings, and shaking each of his friends by the hand in turn. "I have never been so happy. Of course it is sudden: all really delightful things are. And yet it seems to me to be the one thing I have been looking for all my life." He was flushed with excitement and pleasure, and looked extraordinarily handsome.

"I hope you will always be very happy, Dorian," said Hallward, "but I don't quite forgive you for not having let me know of your engagement. You let Harry know."

"And I don't forgive you for being late for dinner," broke in Lord Henry, putting his hand on the lad's shoulder, and smiling as he spoke. "Come, let us sit down and try what the new chef here is like, and then you will tell us how it all came about."

"There is really not much to tell," cried Dorian, as they took their seats at the small round table. "What happened was simply this. After I left you yesterday evening, Harry, I had some dinner at that curious little Italian restaurant in Rupert Street, you introduced me to, and went down afterwards to the theatre. Sibyl was playing Rosalind. Of course the scenery was dreadful, and the Orlando absurd. But Sibyl! You should have seen her! When she came on in the boy's dress she was perfectly wonderful. She wore a moss-coloured velvet jerkin with cinnamon sleeves, slim brown cross-gartered hose, a dainty little green cap with a hawk's feather caught in a jewel, and a hooded cloak lined with dull red. She had never seemed to me more exquisite. She had all the delicate grace of that Tanagra figurine that you have in your studio, Basil. Her hair clustered round her face like dark leaves round a pale rose. As for her acting – well, you will see her to-night. She is simply a born artist. I sat in the dingy box absolutely enthraled. I forgot that I was in London and in the nineteenth century. I was away with my love in a forest that no man had ever seen. After the performance was over I went behind, and spoke to her. As we were sitting together, suddenly there came a look in her eyes that I had never seen there before. My lips moved towards hers. We kissed each other. I can't describe to you what I felt at that moment. I seemed to me that all my life had been narrowed to one perfect point of rose-coloured joy. She trembled all over, and shook like a white narcissus. Then she flung herself on her knees and kissed my hands. I feel that I should not tell you all this, but I can't help it. Of course our engagement is a dead secret. She has not even told her own mother. I don't know what my guardians will say. Lord Radley is sure to be furious. I don't care. I shall be of age in less than a year, and then I can do what I like. I have been right, Basil, haven't I, to take my love out of poetry, and to find my wife in Shakespeare's plays? Lips that Shakespeare taught to speak have whispered their secret in my ear. I have had the arms of Rosalind around me, and kissed Juliet on the mouth."

"Yes, Dorian, I suppose you were right," said Hallward, slowly.

"Have you seen her to-day?" asked Lord Henry.

Dorian Gray shook his head. "I left her in the forest of Arden, I shall find her in an orchard in Verona."

Lord Henry sipped his champagne in a meditative manner. "At what particular point did you mention the word marriage, Dorian? and what did she say in answer? Perhaps you forgot all about it."

"My dear Harry, I did not treat is as a business transaction, and I did not make any formal proposal. I told her that I loved her, and she said she was not worthy to be my wife. Not worthy! Why, the whole world is nothing to me compared to her."

"Women are wonderfully practical," murmured Lord Henry – "much more practical than we are. In situations of that kind we often forget to say anything about marriage, and they always remind us."

Hallward laid his hand upon his arm. "Don't, Harry. You have annoyed Dorian. He is not like other men. He would never bring misery upon any one. His nature is too fine for that."

Lord Henry looked across the table. "Dorian is never annoyed with me," he answered. "I asked the question for the best reason possible, for the only reason, indeed, that excuses one for asking any question – simple curiosity. I have a theory that it is always the women who propose to us, and not we who propose to the women, except, of course, in middle-class life. But then the middle classes are not modern."

Dorian Gray laughed, and tossed his head. "You are quite incorrigible, Harry; but I don't mind. It is impossible to be angry with you. When you see Sibyl Vane you will feel that the man who could wrong her would be a beast without a heart. I cannot understand how any one can wish to shame what he loves. I love Sibyl Vane. I wish to place her on a pedestal of gold, and to see the world worship the woman who is mine. What is marriage? An irrevocable vow. And it is an irrevocable vow that I want to take. Her trust makes me faithful, her belief makes me good. When I am with her, I regret all that you have taught me. I become different from what you have known me to be. I am changed, and the mere touch of Sibyl Vane's hand makes me forget you and all your wrong, fascinating, poisonous, delightful theories."

"You will always like me, Dorian," said Lord Henry. "Will you have some coffee, you fellows? —Waiter, bring coffee, and fine-champagne and some cigarettes. No: don't mind the cigarettes; I have some. —Basil, I can't allow you to smoke cigars. You must have a cigarette. A cigarette is the perfect type of a perfect pleasure. It is exquisite, and it leaves one unsatisfied. What more can you want? —Yes, Dorian, you will always be fond of me. I represent to you all the sins you have never had the courage to commit."

"What nonsense you talk, Harry!" cried Dorian Gray, lighting his cigarette from a fire-breathing silver dragon that the waiter had placed on the table. "Let us go down to the theatre. When you see Sibyl you will have a new ideal of life. She will represent something to you that you have never known."

"I have known everything," said Lord Henry, with a sad look in his eyes, "but I am always ready for a new emotion. I am afraid that there is no such thing, for me at any rate. Still, your wonderful girl may thrill me. Dorian, you will come with me. —I am so sorry, Basil, but there is only room for two in the brougham. You must follow us in the hansom."

They got up and put on their coats, sipping their coffee standing. Hallward was silent and preoccupied. There was a gloom over him. He could not bear this marriage, and yet it seemed to him to be better than many other things that might have happened. After a few moments, they all passed downstairs. He drove off by himself, as had been arranged, and watched the flashing lights of the little brougham in front of him. A strange sense of loss came over him. He felt that Dorian Gray would never again be to him all that he had been in the past. His eyes darkened, and the crowded flaring streets became blurred to him. When the cab drew up the doors of the theatre, it seemed to him that he had grown years older.

FIVE

For some reason or another, the house was crowded that night, and the fat Jew manager who met them at the door was beaming from ear to ear with an oily, tremulous smile. He escorted them to their box with a sort of pompous humility, waving his fat jewelled hands, and talking at the top of his voice. Dorian Gray loathed him more than ever. He felt as if he had come to look for Miranda and had been met by Caliban. Lord Henry, upon the other hand, rather liked him. At least he declared he did, and insisted on shaking him by the hand, and assured him that he was proud to meet a man who had discovered a real genius and gone bankrupt over Shakespeare. Hallward amused himself with watching the faces in the pit. The heat was terribly oppressive, and the huge sunlight flamed like a monstrous dahlia with petals of fire. The youths in the gallery had taken off their coats and waistcoats and hung them over the side. They talked to each other across the theatre, and shared their oranges with the tawdry painted girls who sat by them. Some women were laughing in the pit; their voices were horribly shrill and discordant. The sound of the popping of corks came from the bar.

"What a place to find one's divinity in!" said Lord Henry.

"Yes!" answered Dorian Gray. "It was here I found her, and

she is divine beyond all living things. When she acts you will forget everything. These common people here, with their coarse faces and brutal gestures, become quite different when she is on the stage. They sit silently and watch her. They weep and laugh as she wills them to do. She makes them as responsive as a violin. She spiritualises them, and one feels that they are of the same flesh and blood as one's self."

"Oh, I hope not!" murmured Lord Henry, who was scanning the occupants of the gallery through his opera-glass.

"Don't pay any attention to him, Dorian," said Hallward. "I understand what you mean, and I believe in this girl. Any one you love must be marvellous, and any girl that has the effect you describe must be fine and noble. To spiritualise one's age – that is something worth doing. If this girl can give a soul to those who have lived without one, if she can create a sense of beauty in people whose lives have been sordid and ugly, if she can strip them of their selfishness and lend them tears for sorrows that are not their own, she is worthy of all your adoration, worthy of the adoration of the world. This marriage is quite right. I did not think so at first, but I admit it now. God made Sibyl Vane for you. Without her you would have been incomplete."

"Thanks, Basil," answered Dorian Gray, pressing his hand. "I knew that you would understand me. Harry is so cynical, he terrifies me. But here is the orchestra. It is quite dreadful, but it only lasts for about five minutes. Then the curtain rises, and you will see the girl to whom I am going to give all my life, to whom I have given everything that is good in me."

A quarter of an hour afterwards, amidst an extraordinary turmoil of applause, Sibyl Vane stepped on to the stage. Yes, she was certainly lovely to look at – one of the loveliest creatures, Lord Henry thought, that he had ever seen. There was something of the fawn in her shy grace and startled eyes. A faint blush, like the shadow of a rose in a mirror of silver, came to her cheeks as she glanced at the crowded, enthusiastic house. She stepped back a few paces, and her lips seemed to tremble. Basil Hallward leaped to his feet and began to applaud. Dorian Gray sat motionless, gazing on her, like a man in a dream. Lord Henry peered through his opera-glass, murmuring "Charming! charming!"

The scene was the hall of Capulet's house, and Romeo in his pilgrim's dress had entered with Mercutio and his friends. The band, such as it was, struck up a few bars of music, and the dance began. Through the crowd of ungainly, shabbily-dressed actors, Sibyl Vane moved like a creature from a finer world. Her body swayed, as she danced, as a plant sways in the water. The curves of her throat were like the curves of a white lily. Her hands seemed to be made of cool ivory.

Yet she was curiously listless. She showed no sign of joy when her eyes rested on Romeo. The few lines she had to speak–

> *Good pilgrim, you do wrong your hand too much,*
> *Which mannerly devotion shows in this;*
> *For saints have hands that pilgrim's hands do touch,*
> *And palm to palm is holy palmers' kiss*

–with the brief dialogue that follows, were spoken in a thoroughly artificial manner. The voice was exquisite, but from the point of view of tone it was absolutely false. It was wrong in colour. It took away all the lie from the verse. It made the passion unreal.

Dorian Gray grew pale as he watched her. Neither of his friends dared to say anything to him. She seemed to them to be absolutely incompetent. They were horribly disappointed.

Yet they felt the true test of any Juliet is the balcony scene of the second act. They waited for that. If she failed there, there was nothing in her.

She looked charming as she came out in the moonlight. That could not be denied. But the staginess of her acting was unbearable, and grew worse as she went on. Her gestures became absurdly artificial. She over-emphasised everything that she had to say. The beautiful passage–

> *Thou knowest the mask of night is on my face,*
> *Else would a maiden blush bepaint my cheek*
> *For that which thou hast heard me speak to-night*

–was declaimed with the painful precision of a schoolgirl who has been taught to recite by some second-rate professor of elocution. When she leaned over the balcony and came to those wonderful lines–

> *Although I joy in thee,*
> *I have no joy of this contract to-night:*
> *It is too rash, to unadvised, too sudden;*
> *Too like the lightning, which doth cease to be*
> *Ere one can say, 'It lightens.' Sweet, good-night!*
> *This bud of love by summer's ripening breath*
> *May prove a beauteous flower when next we meet*

–she spoke the words as if they conveyed no meaning to her. It was not nervousness. Indeed, so far from being nervous, she seemed absolutely self-contained. It was simply bad art. She was a complete failure.

Even the common uneducated audience of the pit and gallery lost their interest in the play. They got restless, and began to talk loudly and to whistle. The Jew manager, who was standing at the back of the dress-circle, stamped and swore with rage. The only person unmoved was the girl herself.

When the second act was over there came a storm of hisses, and Lord Henry got up from his chair and put on his coat. "She is quite beautiful, Dorian," he said, "but she can't act. Let us go."

"I am going to see the play through," answered the lad, in a hard, bitter voice. "I am awfully sorry that I have made you waste an evening, Harry. I apologise to both of you."

"My dear Dorian, I should think Miss Vane was ill," interrupted Hallward. "We will come some other night."

"I wish she was ill," he rejoined. "But she seems to be to be simply callous and cold. She has entirely altered. Last night she was a great artist. To-night she is merely a commonplace, mediocre actress."

"Don't talk like that about any one you love, Dorian. Love is a more wonderful thing than art."

"They are both simply forms of imitation," murmured Lord Henry. "But do let us go. Dorian, you must not stay here any longer. It is not good for one's morals to see bad acting. Besides, I don't suppose you will want your wife to act. So what does it matter if she plays Juliet like a wooden doll? She is very lovely, and if she knows as little about life as she does about acting, she will be a delightful experience. There are only two kinds of people who are really fascinating – people who know absolutely everything, and people who know absolutely nothing. Good heavens, my dear boy, don't look so tragic! The secret of remaining young is never to have an emotion that is unbecoming. Come to the club with Basil and myself. We will smoke cigarettes and drink to the beauty of Sibyl Vane. She is beautiful. What more can you want?"

"Please go away, Harry," cried the lad. "I really want to be alone. —Basil, you don't mind my asking you to go? Ah! can't you see that my heart is breaking?" The hot tears came to his eyes. His lips trembled and, rushing to the back of the box, he leaned up against the wall hiding his face in his hands.

"Let us go, Basil," said Lord Henry, with a strange tenderness in his voice; and the two young men passed out together.

A few moments afterwards the footlights flared up, and the curtain rose on the third act. Dorian Gray went back to his seat. He looked pale, and proud, and indifferent. The play dragged on, and seemed interminable. Half of the audience went out, tramping in heavy boots, and laughing. The whole thing was a fiasco. The last act was played to almost empty benches.

As soon as it was over, Dorian Gray rushed behind the scenes into the greenroom. The girl was standing alone there, with a look of triumph on her face. Her eyes were lit with an exquisite fire. There was a radiance about her. Her parted lips were smiling over some secret of their own.

When he entered, she looked at him, and an expression of infinite joy came over her. "How badly I acted to-night, Dorian!" she cried.

"Horribly!" he answered, gazing at her in amazement – "Horribly! It was dreadful. Are you ill? You have no idea what it was. You have no idea what I suffered."

The girl smiled. "Dorian," she answered, lingering over his name with long-drawn music in her voice, as though it were sweeter than honey to the red petals of her lips – "Dorian, you should have understood. But you understand now, don't you?"

"Understand what?" he asked, angrily.

"Why I was so bad to-night. Why I shall always be bad. Why I shall never act well again."

He shrugged his shoulders. "You are ill, I suppose. When you are ill you shouldn't act. You make yourself ridiculous. My friends were bored. I was bored."

She seemed not to listen to him. She was transfigured with joy. An ecstasy of happiness dominated her.

"Dorian, Dorian" she cried, "before I knew you, acting was the one reality of my life. It was only in the theatre that I lived. I thought that it was all true. I was Rosalind one night, and Portia the other. The joy of Beatrice was my joy, and the sorrows of Cordelia were mine also. I believed in everything. The common people who acted with me seemed to me to be godlike. The painted scenes were my world. I knew nothing but shadows, and I thought them real. You came – oh, my beautiful love! – and you freed my soul from prison. You taught me what reality really is. To-night, for the first time in my life, I saw through the hollowness, the sham, the silliness, of the empty pageant in which I had always played. To-night, for the first time, I became conscious that the Romeo was hideous, and old, and painted, that the moonlight in the orchard was false, that the scenery was vulgar, and that the words I had to speak were unreal, were not my words, not what I wanted to say. You had brought me something higher, something of which all art is but a reflection. You have made me understand what love really is. My love! my love! I am sick of shadows. You are more to me than all art ever can be. What have I to do with the puppets of a play? When I came on tonight, I could not understand how it was that everything had gone from me. Suddenly it dawned on my soul what it all meant. The knowledge was exquisite to me. I heard them hissing, and I smiled. What should they know of love? Take me away, Dorian – take me away with you, where we can be quite alone. I hate the stage. I might mimic a passion that I do not feel, but I cannot mimic one that burns me like fire. Oh, Dorian, Dorian, you understand now what it al means? Even if you could do it, it would be profanation for me to play at being in love. You have made me see that."

He flung himself down on the sofa, and turned away his face. "You have killed my love," he muttered.

She looked at him in wonder, and laughed. He made no answer. She came across to him, and stroked his hair with her little fingers. She knelt down and pressed his hands to her lips. He drew them away, and a shudder ran through him.

Then he leaped up, and went to the door. "Yes," he cried, "you have killed my love. You used to stir my imagination. Now you don't even stir my curiosity. You simply produce no effect. I loved you because you were wonderful, because you had genius and intellect, because you realised the dreams of great poets and gave shape and substance to the shadows of art. You have thrown it all away. You are shallow and stupid. My God! how mad I was to love you! What a fool I have been! You are nothing to me now. I will never see you again. I will never think of you. I will never mention your name. You don't know what you were to me, once. Why, once… Oh, I can't bear to think of it! I wish I had never laid eyes upon you! You have spoiled the romance of my life. How little you can know of love, if you say it mars your art! What are you without your art? Nothing. I would have made you famous, splendid, magnificent. The world would have worshipped you, and you would have belonged to me. What are you now? A third-rate actress with a pretty face."

The girl grew white, and trembled. She clenched her hands together and her voice seemed to catch in her throat. "You are not serious, Dorian?" she murmured. "You are acting."

"Acting! I leave that to you. You do it so well," he answered, bitterly.

She rose from her knees, and, with a piteous expression of pain in her face, came across the room to him. She put her hand upon his arm and looked into this eyes. He thrust her back. "Don't touch me!" he cried.

A low moan broke from her, and she flung herself at his feet, and lay there like a trampled flower. "Dorian, Dorian, don't leave me!" she whispered. "I am so sorry I didn't act well. I was thinking of you all the time. But I will try – indeed, I will try. It came so suddenly across me, my love for you. I think I should never have known it if you had not kissed me – if we had not kissed each other. Kiss me again, my love. Don't go away from me. I couldn't bear it. Can't you forgive me for tonight? I will work so hard, and try to improve. Don't be cruel to me because I love you better than anything in the world. After all, it is only once that I have not pleased you. But you are quite right, Dorian. I should have shown myself more of an artist. It was foolish of me; and yet I couldn't help it. Oh, don't leave me, don't leave me." A fit of passionate sobbing choked her. She crouched on the floor like a wounded thing, and Dorian Gray, with his beautiful eyes, looked down at her, and his chiselled lips curled in exquisite disdain. There is always something ridiculous about the passions of people whom one has ceased to love. Sibyl Vane seemed to him to be absurdly melodramatic. Her tears and sobs annoyed him.

"I am going," he said at last, in his calm, clear voice. "I don't wish to be unkind, but I can't see you again. You have disappointed me."

She wept silently, and made no answer, but crept nearer to him. Her little hands stretched blindly out, and appeared to be seeking for him. He turned on his heel, and left the room. In a few moments he was out of the theatre.

Where he went to, he hardly knew. He remembered wandering through dimly-lit streets with gaunt black-shadowed archways and evil-looking houses. Women with hoarse voices and harsh laughter had called after him. Drunkards had reeled by cursing, and chattering to themselves like monstrous apes. He had seen grotesque children huddled upon doorsteps, and had heard shrieks and oaths from gloomy courts.

When the dawn was just breaking, he found himself at Covent Garden. Huge carts filled with nodding lilies rumbled slowly down the polished empty street. The air was heavy with the perfume of the flowers, and their beauty seemed to bring him an anodyne for his pain. He followed into the market, and watched the men unloading their wagons. A white-smocked carter offered him some cherries. He thanked him, wondered why he refused to accept any money for them, and began to eat them listlessly. They had been plucked at midnight, and the coldness of the moon had entered into them. A long line of boys carrying crates of striped tulips, and of yellow and red roses, defiled in front of him, threading their way through the huge jade-green piles of vegetables. Under the portico, with its grey sun-bleached pillars, loitered a troop of draggled bareheaded girls, waiting for the auction to be over. After some time he hailed a hansom and drove home. The sky was pure opal now, and the roofs of the houses glistened like silver against it. As he was passing through the library towards the door of his bedroom his eye fell upon the portrait Basil Hallward had painted of him. He started back in surprise and then went over to it and examined it. In the dim arrested light that struggled through the cream-coloured silk blinds, the face seemed to him to be a little changed. The expression looked different. One would have said that there was a touch of cruelty in the mouth. It was certainly curious.

He turned round, and, walking to the window, drew the blinds up. The bright dawn flooded the room, and swept the fantastic shadows into dusky corners, where they lay shuddering. But the strange expression that he had noticed in the face of the portrait seemed to linger there, to be more intensified even. The quivering, ardent sunlight showed him the lines of cruelty round the mouth as clearly as if he had been looking into a mirror after he had done some dreadful thing.

He winced, and, taking up from the table an oval glass framed in ivory Cupids, that Lord Henry had given him, he glanced hurriedly into it. No line like that warped his red lips. What did it mean?

He rubbed his eyes, and came close to the picture, and examined it again. There were no signs of change when he looked into the actual painting, and yet there was no doubt that the whole expression had altered. It was not a mere fancy of his own. The thing was horribly apparent.

He threw himself into a chair, and began to think. Suddenly there flashed across his mind what he had said in Basil Hallward's studio the day the picture had been finished. Yes, he remembered it perfectly. He had uttered a mad wish that he himself might remain young, and the portrait grow old; that his own beauty might be untarnished, and the face on the canvas bear the burden of his passions and his sins; that the painted image might be seared with the lines of suffering and thought, and that he might keep all the delicate bloom and loveliness of his then just conscious boyhood. Surely his prayer had not been answered? Such things were impossible. It seemed monstrous even to think of them. And, yet, there was the picture before him, with the touch of cruelty in the mouth.

Cruelty! Had he been cruel? It was the girl's fault, not his. He had dreamed of her as a great artist, had given his love to her because he had thought her great. Then she had disappointed him. She had been shallow and unworthy. And, yet, a feeling of infinite regret came over him as he thought of her lying at his feet sobbing like a little child. He remembered with what callousness he had watched her. Why had he been made like that? Why had such a soul been given to him? But he had suffered also. During the last three terrible hours that the play had lasted he had lived centuries of pain, aeon upon aeon of torture. His life was well worth hers. She had marred him for a moment, if he had wounded her for an age. Besides, women were better suited to bear sorrow than men. They lived on their emotions. They only thought of their emotions. When they took lovers, it was merely to have some one with whom they could have scenes. Lord Henry had told him that, and Lord Henry knew what women were. Why should he trouble about Sibyl Vane? She was nothing to him now.

But the picture? What was he to say of that? It held the secret of his life, and told his story. It had taught him to love his own beauty. Would it teach him to loathe his own soul? Would he ever look at it again?

No; it was merely an illusion wrought on the troubled senses. The horrible night that he had passed had left phantoms behind it. Suddenly there had fallen upon his brain that tiny scarlet speck that makes men mad. The picture had not changed. It was folly to think so.

Yet it was watching him, with its beautiful marred face and its cruel smile. Its bright hair gleamed in the early sunlight. Its blue eyes met his own. A sense of infinite pity, not for himself, but for the painted image of himself, came over him. It had altered already, and would alter more. Its gold would wither into gray. Its red and white roses would die. For every sin that he committed, a stain would fleck and wreck its fairness. But he would not sin. The picture, changed or unchanged, would be to him the visible emblem of conscience. He would resist temptation. He would not see Lord Henry any more – would not, at any rate, listen to those subtle poisonous theories that in Basil Hallward's garden had first stirred within him the passion for impossible things. He would go back to Sibyl Vane, make her amends, marry her, try to love her again. Yes, it was his duty to do so. She must have suffered more than he had. Poor child! He had been selfish and cruel to her. The fascination that she had exercised over him would return. They would be happy together. His life with her would be beautiful and pure.

He got up from his chair, and drew a large screen right in front of the portrait, shuddering as he glanced at it. "How horrible!" he murmured to himself, and he walked across to the window and opened it. When he stepped out on the grass, he drew a deep breath. The fresh morning air seemed to drive away all his sombre passions. He thought only of Sibyl Vane. A faint echo of his love came back to him. He repeated her name over and over again. The birds that were singing in the dew-drenched garden seemed to be telling the flowers about her.

SIX

It was long past noon when he awoke. His valet had crept in several times into the room on tiptoe to see if he was stirring, and had wondered what made his young master sleep so late. Finally his bell sounded, and Victor came in softly with a cup of tea, and a pile of letters, on a small tray of old Sèvres china, and drew back the olive-satin curtains, with their shimmering blue lining, that hung in front of the three tall windows.

"Monsieur has well slept this morning," he said smiling.

"What o'clock is it, Victor?" asked Dorian Gray, sleepily.

"One hour and a quarter, monsieur."

How late it was! He sat up, and, having sipped some tea, turned over his letters. One of them was from Lord Henry, and had been brought by hand that morning. He hesitated for a moment, and then put it aside. The others he opened listlessly. They contained the usual collection of cards, invitations to dinner, tickets for private views, programmes of charity concerts, and the like, that are showered on fashionable young men every morning during the season. There was a rather heavy bill, for a chased silver Louis-Quinze toilet-set, that he had not yet had the courage to send on to his guardians, who were extremely old-fashioned people and did not realise that we live in an age when only unnecessary things are absolutely necessary to us; and there were several very courteously worded communications from Jermyn Street money-lenders offering to advance any sum of money at a moment's notice and at the most reasonable rates of interest.

After about ten minutes he got up, and, throwing on an elaborate dressing-gown, passed into the onyx-paved bath-room. The cool water refreshed him after his long sleep. He seemed to have forgotten all that he had gone through. A dim sense of having taken part in some strange tragedy came to him once or twice, but there was the unreality of a dream about it.

As soon as he was dressed, he went into the library and sat down to a light French breakfast, that had been laid out for him on a small round table close to an open window. It was an exquisite day. The warm air seemed laden with spices. A bee flew in, and buzzed around the blue-dragon bowl, filled with sulphur-yellow roses, that stood in front of him. He felt perfectly happy.

Suddenly his eye fell on the screen that he had placed in front of the portrait, and he started.

"Too cold for Monsieur?" asked his valet, putting an omelette on the table. "I shut the window?"

Dorian shook his head. "I am not cold," he murmured.

Was it all true? Had the portrait really changed? Or had it been simply his own imagination that had made him see a look of evil where there had been a look of joy? Surely a painted canvas could not alter? The thing was absurd. It would serve as a tale to tell Basil some day. It would make him smile.

And, yet, how vivid was his recollection of the whole thing! First in the dim twilight, and then in the bright dawn, he had seen the touch of cruelty in the warped lips. He almost dreaded his valet leaving the room. He knew that when he was alone he would have to examine the portrait. He was afraid of certainty. When the coffee and cigarettes had been brought and the man turned to go, he felt a mad desire to tell him to remain. As the door closed behind him he called him back. The man stood waiting for his orders. Dorian looked at him for a moment. "I am not at home to any one, Victor," he said, with a sigh. The man bowed and retired.

He rose from the table, lit a cigarette, and flung himself down on a luxuriously-cushioned couch that stood facing the screen. The screen was an old one of gilt Spanish leather, stamped and wrought with a rather florid Louis-Quatorze pattern. He scanned it curiously, wondering if it had ever before concealed the secret of a man's life.

Should he move it aside, after all? Why not let it stay there? What was the use of knowing? If the thing was true, it was terrible. If it was not true, why trouble about it? But what if, by some fate or deadlier chance, other eyes than his spied behind, and saw the horrible change? What should he do if Basil Hallward came and asked to look at his own picture? He would be sure to do that. No; the thing had to be examined and at once. Anything would be better than this dreadful state of doubt.

He got up, and locked both doors. At least he would be alone when he looked upon the mask of his shame. Then he drew the screen aside, and saw himself face to face. It was perfectly true. The portrait had altered.

As he often remembered afterwards, and always with no small wonder, he found himself at first gazing at the portrait with a feeling of almost scientific interest. That such a chance should have taken place was incredible to him. And yet it was a fact. Was there some subtle affinity between the chemical atoms, that shaped themselves into form and colour on the canvas, and the soul that was within him? Could it be that what that soul thought, they realised? – that what it dreamed, they made true? Or was there some other, more terrible reason? He shuddered, and felt afraid, and, going back to the couch, lay there, gazing at the picture in sickened horror.

One thing, however, he felt that it had done for him. It had made him conscious how unjust, how cruel, he had been to Sibyl Vane. It was not too late to make reparation for that. She could still be his wife. His unreal and selfish love would yield to some higher influence, would be transformed into some nobler passion, and the portrait that Basil Hallward had painted of him would be a guide to him through life, would be to him what holiness was to some, and conscience to others, and the fear of God to us all. There were opiates for remorse, drugs that could lull the moral sense to sleep. But here was a visible symbol of the degradation of sin. Here was an ever-present sign of the ruin men brought upon their souls.

Three o'clock struck, and four, and half-past four, but he did not stir. He was trying to gather up the scarlet threads of life, and to weave them into a pattern; to find his way through the sanguine labyrinth of passion through which he was wandering. He did not know what to do, or what to think. Finally, he went over to the table and wrote a passionate letter to the girl he had loved, imploring her forgiveness, and accusing himself of madness. He covered page after page with wild words of sorrow, and wilder words of pain. There is a luxury in self-reproach. When we blame ourselves we feel that no one else has a right to blame us. It is the confession, not the priest, that gives us absolution. When Dorian Gray had finished the letter, he felt that he had been forgiven.

Suddenly there came a knock to the door, and he heard Lord Henry's voice outside. "My dear Dorian, I must see you. Let me in at once. I can't bear your shutting yourself up like this."

He made no answer at first, but remained quite still. The knocking still continued, and grew louder. Yes, it was better to let Lord Henry in, and to explain to him the new life he was going to lead, to quarrel with him if it became necessary to quarrel, to part if parting was inevitable. He jumped up, and drew the screen hastily across the picture, and unlocked the door.

"I am so sorry for it all, my dear boy," said Lord Henry, coming in. "But you must not think about it too much."

"Do you mean about Sibyl Vane?" asked Dorian.

"Yes, of course," answered Lord Henry, sinking into a chair, and slowly pulling his gloves off. "It is dreadful, from one point of view, but it was not your fault. Tell me, did you go behind and see her after the play was over?"

"Yes."

"I felt sure you had. Did you make a scene with her?"

"It was brutal, Harry - perfectly brutal. But it is all right now. I am not sorry for anything that has happened. It has taught me to know myself better."

"Ah, Dorian, I am so glad you take it in that way! I was afraid I would find you plunged in remorse, and tearing your nice hair."

"I have got through all that," said Dorian, shaking his head, and smiling. "I am perfectly happy now. I know what conscience is, to begin with. It is not what you told me it was. It is the divinest thing in us. Don't sneer at it, Harry, any more - at least not before me. I want to be good. I can't bear the idea of my soul being hideous."

"A very charming artistic basis for ethics, Dorian! I congratulate you on it. But how are you going to begin?"

"By marrying Sibyl Vane."

"Marrying Sibyl Vane!" cried Lord Henry, standing up, and looking at him in perplexed amazement. "But, my dear Dorian—"

"Yes, Harry, I know what you are going to say. Something dreadful about marriage. Don't say it. Don't ever say things of that kind to me again. Two days ago I asked Sibyl to marry me. I am not going to break my word to her. She is to be my wife."

"Your wife! Dorian!... Didn't you get my letter? I wrote to you this morning, and sent the note down, by my own man."

"Your letter? Oh, yes, I remember. I have not read it yet, Harry. I was afraid there might be something in it that I wouldn't like."

Lord Henry walked across the room, and, sitting down by

Dorian Gray, took both his hands in his, and held them tightly. "Dorian," he said, "my letter – don't be frightened – was to tell you that Sibyl Vane is dead."

A cry of pain rose from the lad's lips, and he leapt to his feet, tearing his hands away from Lord Henry's grasp. "Dead! Sibyl dead! It is not true! It is a horrible lie!"

"It is quite true, Dorian," said Lord Henry gravely. "It is in all the morning papers. I wrote down to you to ask you not to see any one till I came. There will have to be an inquest, of course, and you must not be mixed up in it. Things like that make a man fashionable in Paris. But in London people are so prejudiced. Here, one should never make one's debut with a scandal. One should reserve that to give an interest to one's old age. I don't suppose they know your name at the theatre. If they don't, it is all right. Did any one see you going round to her room? That is an important point."

Dorian did not answer for a few moments. He was dazed with horror. Finally he murmured, in a stifled voice, "Harry, did you say an inquest? What did you mean by that? Did Sibyl? – Oh, Harry, I can't bear it! But be quick. Tell me everything at once."

"I have no doubt it was not an accident, Dorian, though it must be put in that way to the public. As she was leaving the theatre with her mother, about half-past twelve or so, she said she had forgotten something up-stairs. They waited some time for her, but she did not come down again. They ultimately found her lying dead on the floor of her dressing-room. She had swallowed something by mistake, some dreadful thing they use at theatres. I don't know what it was, but it had either prussic acid or white lead in it. I should fancy it was prussic acid, as she seems to have died instantaneously. It is very tragic, of course, but you must not get yourself mixed up in it. I see by the 'Standard' that she was seventeen. I should have thought she was almost younger than that. She looked such a child, and seemed to know so little about acting. Dorian, you mustn't let this thing get on your nerves. You must come and dine with me, and afterwards we will look in at the Opera. It is a Patti night, and everybody will be there. You can come to my sister's box. She has got some smart women with her."

"So I have murdered Sibyl Vane," said Dorian Gray, half to himself – "murdered her as certainly as if I had cut her little throat with a knife. And the roses are not less lovely for all that. The birds sing just as happily in my garden. And to-night I am to dine with you, and then go on to the Opera, and sup somewhere I suppose, afterwards. How extraordinarily dramatic life is! If I had read all this in a book, Harry, I think I would have wept over it. Somehow, now that it has happened actually, and to me, it seems far too wonderful for tears. Here is the first passionate love-letter I have ever written in my life. Strange, that my first passionate love-letter should have been addressed to a dead girl. Can they feel, I wonder, those white silent people we call the dead? Sibyl! Can she feel, or know, or listen? Oh, Harry, how I loved her once! It seems years ago to me now. She was everything to me. Then came that dreadful night – was it really only last night? – when she played so badly, and my heart almost broke. She explained it all to me. It was terribly pathetic. But I was not moved a bit. I thought her shallow. Then something happened that made me afraid. I can't tell you what it was, but it was awful. I said I would go back to her. I felt I had done wrong. And now she is dead. My God! my God! Harry, what shall I do? You don't know the danger I am in, and there is nothing to keep me straight. She would have done that for me. She had no right to kill herself. It was selfish of her."

"My dear Dorian, the only way a woman can ever reform a man is by boring him so completely that he loses all possible interest in life. If you had married this girl you would have been wretched. Of course you would have treated her kindly. One can always be kind to people about whom one cares nothing. But she would have soon found out that you were absolutely indifferent to her. And when a woman finds that out about her husband, she either becomes dreadfully dowdy, or wears very smart bonnets that some other woman's husband has to pay for. I say nothing about the social mistake, but I assure you that in any case the whole thing would have been an absolute failure."

"I suppose it would," muttered the lad, walking up and down the room, and looking horribly pale. "But I thought it was my duty. It is not my fault that this terrible tragedy has prevented my doing what was right. I remember your saying once that there is a fatality about good resolutions – that they are always made too late. Mine certainly were."

"Good resolutions are simply a useless attempt to interfere with scientific laws. Their origin is pure vanity. Their result is absolutely nil. They give us, now and then, some of those luxurious sterile emotions that have a certain charm for us. That is all that can be said for them."

"Harry," cried Dorian Gray, coming over and sitting down beside him, "why is it that I cannot feel this tragedy as much as I want to? I don't thing I am heartless. Do you?"

"You have done too many foolish things in your life to be entitled to give yourself that name, Dorian," answered Lord Harry, with his sweet, melancholy smile.

The lad frowned. "I don't like that explanation, Harry," he rejoined, "but I am glad you don't think I am heartless. I am nothing of the kind. I know I am not. And yet I must admit that this thing that has happened does not affect me as it should. It seems to me to be simply like a wonderful ending to a wonderful play. It has all the terrible beauty of a great tragedy, in which I took part, a tragedy, but by which I have not been wounded."

"It is an interesting question," said Lord Henry, who found an exquisite pleasure in playing on the lad's unconscious egotism – "an extremely interesting question. I fancy that the explanation is this. It often happens that the real tragedies of life occur in such an inartistic manner that they hurt us by their crude violence, their absolute incoherence, their absurd want of meaning, their entire lack of style. They affect us just as vulgarity affects us. They give us an impression of sheer brute force, and we revolt against that. Sometimes, however, a tragedy that has artistic elements of beauty crosses our lives. If these elements of beauty are real the whole thing simply appeals of our sense of dramatic effect. Suddenly we find that we are no longer the actors but the spectators of the play. Or rather we are both. We watch ourselves, and the mere wonder of the spectacle enthrals us. In the present case, what is it that has really happened? Some one has killed herself for love of you. I wish I had ever had such an experience. It would have made me in love with love for the rest of my life. The people who have adored me – there have not been very many, but there have been some – have always insisted on living on, long after I had ceased to care for them, or they to care for me. They have become stout and tedious, and when I meet them they go in at once for reminiscences. That awful memory of woman! What a fearful thing it is! And what an utter intellectual stagnation it reveals! One should absorb the colour of life, but one should never remember its details. Details are always vulgar.

"Of course, now and then things linger. I once wore nothing but violcts all through onc scason, as mourning for a romance that would not die. I forget what killed it. I think it was her proposing to sacrifice the whole world for me. That is always a dreadful moment. It fills one with the terror of eternity. Well – would you believe it? – a week ago, at Lady Hampshire's, I found myself seated at dinner next to the lady in question, and she insisted on going over the whole thing again, and digging up the past, and raking up the future. I had buried my romance in a bed of poppies. She dragged it out again, and assured me that I had spoiled her life. I am bound to state that she ate an enormous dinner, so I did not feel any anxiety. But what a lack of taste she showed! The one charm of the past is that it is the past. But women never know when the curtain has fallen. They always want a sixth act, and as soon as the interest of the play is entirely over they propose to continue it. If they were allowed to have their way, every comedy would have a tragic ending, and every tragedy would culminate in a farce. They are charmingly artificial, but they have no sense of art. You are more fortunate than I am. I assure you, Dorian, that not one of the women I have known would have done for me what Sibyl Vane did for you. Ordinary women always console themselves. Some of them do it by going in for sentimental colours. Never trust a woman who wears mauve, whatever her age may be, or a woman over thirty-five who is fond of pink ribbons. It always means that they have a history. Others find a great consolation in suddenly discovering the good qualities in their husbands. They flaunt their conjugal felicity in one's face, as if it was the most fascinating of sins. Religion consoles some. Its mysteries have all the charm of a flirtation, a woman once told me; and I can quite understand it. Besides, nothing makes one so vain as being told that one is a sinner. There is really no end to the consolations that women find in modern life. Indeed, I have not mentioned the most important one of all."

"What is that, Harry?" said Dorian Gray, listlessly.

"Oh, the obvious one. Taking some one else's admirer when one loses one's own. In good society that always whitewashes a woman. But really, Dorian, how different Sibyl Vane must have been from all the women one meets! There is something to me quite beautiful about her death. I am glad I am living in a century when such wonders happen. They make one believe in the reality of the things that shallow, fashionable people play with, such as romance, passion, and love."

"I was terribly cruel to her. You forget that."

"I believe that women appreciate cruelty more than anything else. They have wonderfully primitive instincts. We have emancipated them but they remain slaves looking for their masters, all the same. They love being dominated. I am sure you were splendid. I have never seen you angry, but I can fancy how delightful you looked. And, after all, you said something to me the day before yesterday that seemed to me at the time to be merely fanciful, but that I see now was absolutely true, and it explains everything."

"What was that, Harry?"

"You said to me that Sibyl Vane represented to you all the heroines of romance – that she was Desdemona one night, and Ophelia the other; that if she died as Juliet, she came to life as Imogen."

"She will never come to life again now," murmured the lad, burying his face in his hands.

"No, she will never come to life. She has played her last part. But you must think of that lonely death in the tawdry dressing-room simply as a strange lurid fragment from some Jacobean tragedy, as a wonderful scene from Webster, or Ford, or Cyril Tourneur. The girl never really lived, and so she has never really died. To you at least she was always a dream, a phantom that flitted through Shakespeare's plays and left them lovelier for its presence, a reed through which Shakespeare's music sounded richer and more full of joy. The moment she touched actual life, she marred it, and it marred her, and so she passed away. Mourn for Ophelia, if you like. Put ashes on your head because Cordelia was strangled. Cry out against Heaven because the daughter of Brabantio died. But don't waste your tears over Sibyl Vane. She was less real then they are."

There was a silence. The evening darkened in the room. Noiselessly and with silver feet, the shadows crept in from the garden. The colours faded wearily out of things.

After some time Dorian Gray looked up. "You have explained me to myself, Harry," he murmured, with something of a sigh of relief. "I felt all that you have said, but somehow I was afraid of it, and I could not express myself. How well you know me! But we will not talk again of what has happened. It has been a marvellous experience. That is all. I wonder if life has still in store for me anything as marvellous."

"Life has everything in store for you, Dorian. There is nothing that you, with your extraordinary good looks, will not be able to do."

"But suppose, Harry, I became haggard, and gray, and wrinkled? What then?"

"Ah, then," said Lord Henry, rising to go – "then my dear Dorian, you would have to fight for your victories. As it is, they are brought to you. No, you must keep your good looks. We live in an age that reads too much to be wise, and that thinks too must to be beautiful. We cannot spare you. And now you had better dress, and drive down to the club. We are rather late, as it is."

"I think I shall join you at the Opera, Harry. I feel too tired to eat anything. What is the number of your sister's box?"

"Twenty-seven, I believe. It is on the grand tier. You will see her name on the door. But I am sorry you won't come and dine."

"I don't feel up to it," said Dorian, wearily. "But I am awfully obliged to you for all that you have said to me. You are certainly my best friend. No one has ever understood me as you have."

"We are only at the beginning of our friendship, Dorian," answered Lord Henry, shaking him by the hand. "Good-bye. I shall see you before nine-thirty, I hope. Remember, Patti is singing."

As he closed the door behind him, Dorian Gray touched the bell, and in a few minutes Victor appeared with the lamps and drew the blinds down. He waited impatiently for him to go. The man seemed to take an interminable time about everything.

As soon as he had left, he rushed to the screen, and drew it back. No; there was no further change in the picture. It had received the news of Sibyl Vane's death before he had known of it himself. It was conscious of the events of life as they occurred. The vicious cruelty that marred the fine lines of the mouth had, no doubt, appeared at the very moment that the girl had drunk the poison, whatever it was. Or was it indifferent to the results? Did it merely take cognisance of what passed within the soul? He wondered, and hoped that some day he would see the change taking place before his very eyes, shuddering as he hoped it.

Poor Sibyl! what a romance it had all been! She had often mimicked death on the stage, and at last Death himself had touched her, and brought her with him. How had she played that dreadful scene? Had she cursed him, as she died? No; she had died for love of him, and love would always be a sacrament to him now. She had atoned for everything, by the sacrifice she had made of her life. He would not think any more of what she had made him go through, that horrible night at the theatre. When he thought of her, it would be as a wonderful tragic figure to show Love had been a great reality. A wonderful tragic figure? Tears came to his eyes as he remembered her child-like look and winsome fanciful ways and shy tremulous grace. He wiped them away hastily, and looked again at the picture.

He felt that the time had really come for making his choice. Or had his choice already been made? Yes, life had decided that for him – life, and his own infinite curiosity about life. Eternal youth, infinite passion, pleasures subtle and secret, wild joys and wilder sins – he was to have all these things. The portrait was to bear the burden of his shame: that was all.

A feeling of pain came over him as he thought of the desecration that was in store for the fair face on the canvas. Once, in boyish mockery of Narcissus, he had kissed, or feigned to kiss, those painted lips that now smiled so cruelly at him. Morning after morning he had sat before the portrait wondering at its beauty, almost enamoured of it, as it seemed to him at times. Was it to alter now with every mood to which he yielded? Was it to become a hideous and loathsome thing, to be hidden away in a locked room, to be shut out from the sunlight that had so often touched to brighter gold the waving wonder of the hair? The pity of it! the pity of it!

For a moment he thought of praying that the horrible sympathy that existed between him and the picture might cease. It had changed in answer to a prayer; perhaps in answer to a prayer it might remain unchanged. And, yet, who, that knew anything about Life, would surrender the chance of remaining always young, however fantastic that chance might be, or with what fateful consequences it might be fraught? Besides, was it really under his control? Had it indeed been prayer that had produced the substitution? Might there not be some curious scientific reason for it all? If thought could exercise its influence upon a living organism, might not thought exercise an influence upon dead and inorganic things? Nay, without thought or conscious desire, might not things external to ourselves vibrate in unison with our moods and passions, atom calling to atom, in secret love or strange affinity? But the reason was of no importance. He would never again tempt by a prayer any terrible power. If the picture was to alter, it was to alter. That was all. Why inquire too closely into it?

For there would be real pleasure in watching it. He would be able to follow his mind into its secret places. This portrait would be to him the most magical of mirrors. As it had revealed to him his own body, so it would reveal to him his own soul. And when winter came upon it he would still be standing where spring trembles on the verge of summer. When the blood crept from its face, and left behind a pallid mask of chalk with leaden eyes, he would keep the glamour of boyhood. Not one blossom of his loveliness would ever fade. Not one pulse of his life would ever weaken. Like the gods of the Greeks, he would be strong, and fleet, and joyous. What did it matter what happened to the coloured image on the canvas? He would be safe. That was everything.

He drew the screen back into its former place in front of the picture, smiling as he did so, and passed into his bedroom, where his valet was already waiting for him. An hour later he was at the Opera, and Lord Henry was leaning over his chair.

SEVEN

As he was sitting at breakfast next morning, Basil Hallward was shown into the room.

"I am so glad I have found you, Dorian," he said gravely. "I called last night, and they told me you were at the Opera. Of course I knew that was impossible. But I wish you had left word where you had really gone to. I passed a dreadful evening, half afraid that one tragedy might be followed by another. I think you might have telegraphed for me when you heard of it first. I read of it quite by chance in a late edition of the 'Globe' that I picked up at the club. I came here at once, and was miserable at not finding you. I can't tell you how heart-broken I am about the whole thing. I know what you must suffer. But where were you? Did you go down and see the girl's mother? For a moment I thought of following you there. They gave the address in the paper. Some where in the Euston Road, isn't it? But I was afraid of intruding upon a sorrow that I could not lighten. Poor woman! What a state she must be in! And her only child, too! What did she say about it all?"

"My dear Basil, how do I know?" murmured Dorian, sipping some pale-yellow wine from a delicate gold-beaded bubble of Venetian glass, and looking dreadfully bored. "I was at the Opera. You should have come on there. I met Lady Gwendolen, Harry's sister, for the first time. We were in her box. She is perfectly charming; and Patti sang divinely. Don't talk about horrid subjects. If one doesn't talk about a thing, it has never happened. It is simply expression, as Harry says, that gives reality to things. Tell me about yourself and what you are painting."

"You went to the Opera?" said Hallward, speaking very slowly, and with a strained touch of pain in his voice. "You went to the Opera while Sibyl Vane was lying dead in some sordid lodging? You can talk to me of other women being charming, and of Patti singing divinely, before the girl you loved has even the quiet of a grave to sleep in? Why, man, there are horrors in store for that little white body of hers!"

"Stop, Basil! I won't hear it!" cried Dorian, leaping to his feet. "You must not tell me about things. What is done is done. What is past is past."

"You call yesterday the past?"

"What has the actual lapse of time got to do with it? It is only shallow people who require years to get rid of an emotion. A man who is master of himself can end a sorrow as easily as he can invent a pleasure. I don't want to be at the mercy of my emotions. I want to use them, to enjoy them, and to dominate them."

"Dorian, this is horrible! Something has changed you completely. You look exactly the same wonderful boy who used to come down to my studio, day after day, to sit for his picture. But you were simple, natural, and affectionate then. You were the most unspoiled creature in the whole world. Now, I don't know what has come over you. You talk as if you had no heart, no pity in you. It is all Harry's influence. I see that."

The lad flushed up, and, going to the window, looked out on the green, flickering garden for a few moments. "I owe a great deal to Harry, Basil," he said, at last – "more than I owe to you. You only taught me to be vain."

"Well, I am punished for that, Dorian – or shall be some

day."

"I don't know what you mean, Basil," he exclaimed, turning round. "I don't know what you want. What do you want?"

"I want the Dorian Gray I used to know."

"Basil," said the lad, going over to him, and putting his hand on his shoulder, "you have come too late. Yesterday, when I heard that Sibyl Vane had killed herself—"

"Killed herself! Good heavens! is there no doubt about that?" cried Hallward, looking up at him with an expression of horror.

"My dear Basil! Surely you don't think it was a vulgar accident? Of course she killed herself. It is one of the great romantic tragedies of the age. As a rule, people who act lead the most commonplace lives. They are good husbands, or faithful wives, or something tedious. You know what I mean – middle-class virtue, and all that kind of thing. How different Sibyl was! She lived her finest tragedy. She was always a heroine. The last night she played – the night you saw her – she acted badly because she had known the reality of love. When she knew its unreality, she died, as Juliet might have died. She passed again into the sphere of art. There is something of the martyr about her. Her death has all the pathetic uselessness of martyrdom, all its wasted beauty. But, as I was saying, you must not think I have not suffered. If you had come in yesterday at a particular moment – about half-past five, perhaps, or a quarter to six – you would have found me in tears. Even Harry, who was here, who brought me the news, in fact, had no idea what I was going through. I suffered immensely, then it passed away. I cannot repeat an emotion. No one can, except sentimentalists. And you are awfully unjust, Basil. You come down here to console me. That is charming of you. You find me consoled, and you are furious. How like a sympathetic person! You remind me of a story Harry told me about a certain philanthropist who spent twenty years of his life in trying to get some grievance redressed, or some unjust law altered

– I forget exactly what it was. Finally he succeeded, and nothing could exceed his disappointment. He had absolutely nothing to do, almost died of ennui, and became a confirmed misanthrope. And besides, my dear old Basil, if you really want to console me, teach me rather to forget what has happened, or to see it from a proper artistic point of view. Was it not Gautier who used to write about 'la consolation des arts'? I remember picking up a little vellum-covered book in your studio one day and chancing on that delightful phrase. Well, I am not like that young man you told me of when we were down at Marlowe together, the young man who used to say that yellow satin could console one for all the miseries of life. I love beautiful things that one can touch and handle. Old brocades, green bronzes, lacquer-work, carved ivories, exquisite surroundings, luxury, pomp – there is much to be got from all these. But the artistic temperament that they create, or at any rate reveal, is still more to me. To become the spectator of one's own life, as Harry says, is to escape the suffering of life. I know you are surprised at my talking to you like this. You have not realised how I have developed. I was a school-boy when you knew me. I am a man now. I have new passions, new thoughts, new ideas. I am different, but you must not like me less. I am changed, but you must always be my friend. Of course I am very fond of Harry. But I know that you are better than he is. You are not stronger – you are too much afraid of life – but you are better. And how happy we used to be together! Don't leave me, Basil, and don't quarrel with me. I am what I am. There is nothing more to be said."

Hallward felt strangely moved. Rugged and straight-forward as he was, there was something in his nature that was purely feminine in its tenderness. The lad was infinitely dear to him, and his personality had been the great turning-point in his art. He could not bear the idea of reproaching him any more. After all, his indifference was probably merely a mood that would pass away. There was so much in him that was good, so much in him that was noble.

"Well, Dorian," he said, at length, with a sad smile, "I won't speak to you again about this horrible thing, after to-day. I only trust your name won't be mentioned in connection with it. The inquest is to take place this afternoon. Have they summonsed you?"

Dorian shook his head, and a look of annoyance passed over his face at the mention of the word 'inquest'. There was something so crude and vulgar about everything of the kind. "They don't know my name," he answered.

"But surely she did?"

"Only my Christian name, and that I am quite sure she never mentioned to any one. She told me once that they were all rather curious to learn who I was, and that she invariably told them my name was Prince Charming. It was pretty of her. You must do me a drawing of her, Basil. I should like to have something more of her than the memory of a few kisses and some broken pathetic words."

"I will try and do something, Dorian, if it would please you. But you must come and sit to me yourself again. I can't get on without you."

"I will never sit to you again, Basil. It is impossible!" he exclaimed, starting back.

Hallward stared at him, "My dear boy, what nonsense!" he cried. "Do you mean to say you don't like what I did of you? Where is it? Why have you pulled the screen in front of it? Let me look at it. It is the best thing I have ever painted. Do take that screen away, Dorian. It is simply horrid of your servant hiding my work like that. I felt the room looked different as I came in."

"My servant has nothing to do with it, Basil. You don't imagine I let him array my room for me? He settles my flowers for me sometimes - that is all. No; I did it myself. The light was too strong on the portrait."

"Too strong! Impossible, my dear fellow! It is an admirable place for it. Let me see it." And Hallward walked towards the corner of the room.

A cry of terror broke from Dorian Gray's lips, and he rushed between Hallward and the screen. "Basil," he said, looking very pale, "you must not look at it. I don't wish you to."

"Not look at my own work! you are not serious. Why shouldn't I look at it?" exclaimed Hallward, laughing.

"If you try to look at it, Basil, on my word of honour I will never speak to you again as long as I live. I am quite serious. I don't offer any explanation, and you are not to ask for any. But, remember, if you touch this screen, everything is over between us."

Hallward was thunderstruck. He looked at Dorian Gray in absolute amazement. He had never seen him like this before. The lad was absolutely pallid with rage. His hands were clinched, and the pupils of his eyes were like disks of blue fire. He was trembling all over.

"Dorian!"

"Don't speak!"

"But what is the matter? Of course I won't look at it if you don't want me to," he said, rather coldly, turning on his heel, and going over towards the window. "But, really, it seems rather absurd that I shouldn't see my own work, especially as I am going to exhibit it in Paris in the autumn. I shall probably have to give it another coat of varnish before that, so I must see it some day, and why not to-day?"

"To exhibit it! You want to exhibit it?" exclaimed Dorian Gray, a strange sense of terror creeping over him. Was the world going to be shown his secret? Were people to gape at the mystery of his life? That was impossible. Something – he did not know what – had to be done at once.

"Yes: I don't suppose you will object to that. Georges Petit is going to collect all my best pictures for a special exhibition in the Rue de Sèze, which will open the first week in October. The portrait will only be away a month. I should think you could easily spare it for that time. In fact, you are sure to be out of town. And if you hide it always behind a screen, you can't care much about it."

Dorian Gray passed his hand over his forehead. There were beads of perspiration there. He felt that he was on the brink of a horrible danger. "You told me a month ago that you would never exhibit it," he said. "Why have you changed your mind? You people who go in for being consistent have just as many moods as others. The only difference is that your moods are rather meaningless. You can't have forgotten that you assured me most solemnly that nothing in the world would induce you to send it to any exhibition. You told Harry exactly the same thing." He stopped suddenly, and a gleam of light came into his eyes. He remembered that Lord Henry had said to him once, half seriously and half in jest, "If you want to have an interesting quarter of an hour, get Basil to tell you why he won't exhibit your picture. He told me why he wouldn't, and it was a revelation to me." Yes, perhaps Basil, too, had his secret. He would ask him and try.

"Basil," he said, coming over quite close, and looking him straight in the face, "we have each of us a secret. Let me know yours, and I will tell you mine. What was your reason for refusing to exhibit my picture?"

Hallward shuddered in spite of himself. "Dorian, if I told you, you might like me less than you do, and you would certainly laugh at me. I could not bear your doing either of those two things. If you wish me never to look at your picture again, I am content. I have always you to look at. If you wish the best work I have ever done to be hidden from the world, I am satisfied. Your friendship is dearer to me than any fame or reputation."

"No, Basil, you must tell me," murmured Dorian Gray. "I think I have a right to know." His feeling of terror had passed away, and curiosity had taken its place. He was determined to find out Basil Hallward's mystery.

"Let us sit down, Dorian," said Hallward, looking pale and pained. "Let us sit down. I will sit in the shadow, and you shall sit in the sunlight. Our lives are like that. Just answer me one question. Have you noticed in the picture something that you did not like? – something that probably at first did not strike you, but that revealed itself to you suddenly?"

"Basil!" cried the lad, clutching the arms of his chair with trembling hands, and gazing at him with wild, startling eyes.

"I see you did. Don't speak. Wait till you hear what I have to say. It is quite true that I have worshipped you with far more romance of feeling than a man usually gives to a friend. Somehow, I had never loved a woman. I suppose I never had time. Perhaps, as Harry says, a really 'grande passion' is the privilege of those who have nothing to do, and that is the use of the idle classes in a country. Well, from the moment I met you, your personality had the most extraordinary influence over me. I quite admit that I adored you madly, extravagantly, absurdly. I was jealous of every one to whom you spoke. I wanted to have you all to myself. I was only happy when I was with you. When I was away from you, you were still present in my art. It was all wrong and foolish still. Of course I never let you know anything about this. It would have been impossible. You would not have understood it; I did not understand it myself. One day I determined to paint a wonderful portrait of you. It was to have been my masterpiece. It is my masterpiece. But, as I worked at it, every flake and film of colour seemed to me to reveal my secret. I grew afraid that the world would know of my idolatry. I felt, Dorian, that I had told too much. Then it was that I resolved never to allow the picture to be exhibited. You were a little annoyed; but then you did not realise all that it meant to me. But I did not mind that. When the picture was finished, and I sat alone with it, I felt that I was right. Well, after a few days the portrait left my studio, and as soon as I had got rid of the intolerable fascination of its presence it seemed to me that I had been foolish in imagining that I had said anything in it, more than that you were extremely good-looking and that I could paint. Even now I cannot help feeling that it is a mistake to think that the passion one feels in creation is ever really shown in the work one creates. Art is more abstract than we fancy. Form and colour tell us of form and colour – that is all. It often seems to me that art conceals the artist far more completely than it ever reveals him. And so when I got this offer from Paris I determined to make your portrait the principal thing in my exhibition. It never occurred to me that you would refuse. I see now that you were right. The picture must not be shown. You must not be angry with me, Dorian, for what I have told you. As I said to Harry, once, you are made to be worshipped."

Dorian Gray drew a long breath. The colour came back to his cheeks, and a smile played about his lips. The peril was over. He was safe for the time. Yet he could not help feeling infinite pity for the young man who had just made this strange confession to him. He wondered if he would ever be so dominated by the personality of a friend. Lord Harry had all the charm of being very dangerous. But that was all. He was too clever and too cynical to be really fond of. Would there ever be some one who would fill him with a strange idolatry? Was that one of the things that life had in store?

"It is extraordinary to me, Dorian," said Hallward, "that you should have seen this in the picture. Did you really see it?"

"Of course I did."

"Well, you don't mind my looking at it now?"

Dorian shook his head. "You must not ask me that, Basil. I could not possibly let you stand in front of that picture."

"You will some day, surely?"

"Never."

"Well, perhaps you are right. And now good-bye, Dorian. You have been the one person in my life of whom I have been really fond. I don't suppose I shall often see you again. You don't know what it cost me to tell you all that I have told you."

"My dear Basil," cried Dorian, "what have you told me? Simply that you felt that you like me too much. That is not even a compliment."

"It was not intended as a compliment. It was a confession."

"A very disappointing one."

"Why, what did you expect, Dorian? You didn't see anything else in the picture, did you? There was nothing else to see?"

"No: there was nothing else to see. Why do you ask? But you mustn't talk about not meeting me again, or anything of that kind. You and I are friends, Basil, and we must always remain so."

"You have got Harry," said Hallward, sadly.

"Oh, Harry!" cried the lad, with a ripple of laughter. "Harry spends his days in saying what is incredible, and his evenings in doing what is improbable. Just the sort of life I would like to lead. But still I don't think I would go to Harry if I was in trouble. I would sooner go to you, Basil."

"But you won't sit to me again?"

"Impossible!"

"You spoil my life as an artist by refusing, Dorian. No man comes across two ideal things. Few come across one."

"I can't explain it to you, Basil, but I must never sit to you again. I will come and have tea with you. That will be just as pleasant."

"Pleasanter for you, I am afraid," murmured Hallward, regretfully. "And now good-bye. I am sorry you won't let me look at the picture once again. But that can't be helped. I quite understand what you feel about it."

As he left the room, Dorian Gray smiled to himself. Poor Basil! How little he knew of the true reason! And how strange it was that, instead of having been forced to reveal his own secret, he had succeeded, almost by chance, in wresting a secret from his friend! How much that strange confession explained to him! Basil's absurd fits of jealousy, his wild devotion, his extravagant panegyrics, his curious reticences – he understood them all now, and he felt sorry. There was something tragic in a friendship so coloured by romance.

He sighed, and touched the bell. The portrait must be hidden away at all costs. He could not run such a risk of discovery again. It had been mad of him to have the thing remain, even for an hour, in a room to which any of his friends had access.

EIGHT

When his servant entered, he looked at him steadfastly, and wondered if he had thought of peering behind the screen. The man was quite impassive, and waited for his orders. Dorian lit a cigarette, and walked over to the glass and glanced into it. He could see the reflection of Victor's face perfectly. It was like a placid mask of servility. There was nothing to be afraid of, there. Yet he thought it best to be on his guard.

Speaking very slowly, he told him to tell the housekeeper that he wanted to see her, and then to go to the frame-maker's and ask him to send two of his men round at once. It seemed to him that as the man left the room he peered in the direction of the screen. Or was that only his fancy?

After a few moments, Mrs. Leaf, a dear old lady in a black silk dress with a photograph of the late Mr. Leaf framed in a large gold brooch at her neck, and old-fashioned thread mittens on her wrinkled hands, bustled into the room.

"Well, Master Dorian," she said, "what can I do for you? I beg your pardon, sir," – here came a courtesy – "I shouldn't call you Master Dorian any more. But, Lord bless you, sir, I have known you since you were a baby, and many's the trick you've played on poor old Leaf. Not that you were not always a good boy, sir; but boys will be boys, Master Dorian, and jam is a temptation to the young, isn't it, sir?"

He laughed. "You must always call me Master Dorian, Leaf. I will be very angry with you if you don't. And I assure you I am quite as fond of jam now as I used to be. Only when I am asked out to tea I am never offered any. I want you to give me the key of the room at the top of the house."

"The old school-room, Master Dorian? Why, it's full of dust. I must get it arranged and put straight before you go into it. It's not fit for you to see, Master Dorian. It is not, indeed."

"I don't want it put straight, Leaf. I only want the key."

"Well, Master Dorian, you'll be covered with cobwebs if you goes into it. Why, it hasn't been opened for nearly five years – not since his lordship died."

He winced at the mention of his dead uncle's name. He had hateful memories of him. "That does not matter, Leaf," he replied. "All I want is the key."

"And here is the key, Master Dorian," said the old lady, after going over the contents of her bunch with tremulously uncertain hands. "Here is the key. I'll have it off the ring in a moment. But you don't think of living up there, Master Dorian, and you so comfortable here?"

"No, Leaf, I don't. I merely want to see the place, and perhaps store something in it – that is all. Thank you, Leaf. I hope your rheumatism is better; and mind you send me up jam for breakfast."

Mrs. Leaf shook her head. "Them foreigners doesn't understand jam, Master Dorian. They calls it 'compot'. But I'll bring it to you myself some morning, if you lets me."

"That will be very kind of you, Leaf," he answered, looking at the key; and having made him an elaborate courtesy, the old lady left the room, her face wreathed in smiles. She had a strong objection to the French valet. It was a poor thing, she felt, for any one to be born a foreigner.

As the door closed, Dorian put the key in his pocket, and looked round the room. His eye fell on a large purple satin coverlet heavily embroidered with gold, a splendid piece of late seventeenth-century Venetian work that his uncle had found in a convent near Bologna. Yes, that would serve to wrap the dreadful thing in. It had perhaps served often as a pall for the dead. Now it was to hide something that had a corruption of its own, worse than the corruption of death itself – something that would breed horrors and yet would never die. What the worm was to the corpse, his sins would be to the painted image on the canvas. They would mar its beauty, and eat away its grace. They would defile it, and make it shameful. And yet the thing would still live on. It would be always alive.

He shuddered, and for a moment he regretted that he had not told Basil the true reason why he had wished to hide the picture away. Basil would have helped him to resist Lord Henry's influence, and the still more poisonous influences that came from his own temperament. The love that he bore him – for it was really love – had something noble and intellectual in it. It was not that mere physical admiration of beauty that is born of the senses, and that dies when the senses tire. It was such love as Michael Angelo had known, and Montaigne, and Winckelmann, and Shakespeare himself. Yes, Basil could have saved him. But it was too late now. The past could always be annihilated. Regret, denial, or forgetfulness could do that. But the future was inevitable. There were passions in him that would find their terrible outlet, dreams that would make the shadow of their evil real.

He took up from the couch the great purple-and-gold texture that covered it, and, holding it in his hands, passed behind the screen. Was the face on the canvas viler than before? It seemed to him that it was unchanged; and yet his loathing of it was intensified. Gold hair, blue eyes, and rose-red lips – they all were there. It was simply the expression that had altered. That was horrible in its cruelty. Compared to what he saw in it of censure or rebuke, how shallow Basil's reproaches about Sibyl Vane had been! – how shallow, and of what little account! His own soul was looking out at him from the canvas and calling him to judgment. A look of pain came across him, and he flung the rich pall over the picture. As he did so, a knock came to the door. He passed out as his servant entered.

"The persons are here, monsieur."

He felt that the man must be got rid of at once. He must not be allowed to know where the picture was being taken to. There was something sly about him, and he thought, treacherous eyes. Sitting down at the writing-table, he scribbled a note to Lord Henry, asking him to send round something to read, and reminding him that they were to meet at eight-fifteen that evening.

"Wait for an answer," he said, handing it to him, "and show the men in here."

In two or three minutes there was another knock, and Mr. Ashton himself, the celebrated frame-maker of South Audley Street, came in with a somewhat rough-looking young assistant. Mr. Ashton was a florid, red-whiskered little man, whose admiration for art was considerably tempered by the inveterate impecuniosity of most of the artists who dealt with him. As a rule, he never left his shop. He waited for people to come to him. But he always made an exception in favour of Dorian Gray. There was something about Dorian that charmed everybody. It was a pleasure even to see him.

"What can I do for you, Mr. Gray?" he said, rubbing his fat freckled hands. "I thought I would do myself the honour of coming round in person. I have just got a beauty of a frame, sir. Picked it up at a sale. Old Florentine. Came from Fonthill, I believe. Admirably suited for a religious picture, Mr. Gray."

"I am so sorry you have given yourself the trouble of coming round, Mr. Ashton. I will certainly drop in and look at the frame – though I don't go in much for religious art – but to-day I only want a picture carried to the top of the house for me. It is rather heavy, so I thought I would ask you to lend me a couple of your men."

"No trouble at all, Mr. Gray. I am delighted to be of any service to you. Which is the work of art, sir?"

"This," replied Dorian, moving the screen back. "Can you move it covering and all, just as it is? I don't want it to get scratched going upstairs."

"There will be no difficulty, sir," said the genial frame-maker, beginning, with the aid of his assistant, to unhook the picture from the long brass chains by which it was suspended. "And, now, where shall we carry it to, Mr. Gray?"

"I will show you the way, Mr. Ashton, if you will kindly follow me. Or perhaps you had better go in front. I am afraid it is right at the top of the house. We will go up by the front staircase, as it is wider."

He held the door open for them, and they passed out into the hall and began the ascent. The elaborate character of the frame had made the picture extremely bulky, and now and then, in spite of the obsequious protests of Mr. Ashton, who had a true tradesman's dislike of seeing a gentleman doing anything useful, Dorian put his hand to it so as to help them.

"Something of a load to carry, sir," gasped the little man, when they reached the top landing. And he wiped his shiny forehead.

"A terrible load to carry," murmured Dorian, as he unlocked the door that opened into the room that was to keep for him the curious secret of his life and hide his soul from the eyes of men.

He had not entered the place for more than four years – not, indeed, since he had used it first as a playroom when he was a child and then as a study when he grew somewhat older. It was a large, well-proportioned room, which had been specially built by the last Lord Sherard for the use of the little nephew whom, being himself childless, and perhaps for other reasons, he had always hated and desired to keep at a distance. It did not appear to Dorian to have much changed. There was the huge Italian 'cassone', with its fantastically-painted panels and its tarnished gilt mouldings, in which he had so often hidden himself as a boy. There was the satinwood bookcase filled with his dog-eared school-books. On the wall behind it was hanging the same ragged Flemish tapestry where a faded king and queen were playing chess in a garden, while a company of hawkers rode by, carrying hooded birds of their gauntleted wrists. How well he recalled it all! Every moment of his lonely childhood came back to him, as he looked round. He remembered the stainless purity of his boyish life, and it seemed horrible to him that it was here that the fatal portrait was to be hidden away. How little he had thought, in those dead days, of all that was in store for him!

But there was no other place in the house to secure from prying eyes as this. He had the key, and no one else could enter it. Beneath its purple pall, the face painted on the canvas could grow bestial, sodden, and unclean. What did it matter? No one could see it. He himself would not see it. Why should he watch the hideous corruption of his soul? He kept his youth - that was enough. And, besides, might not his nature grow finer, after all? There was no reason that the future should be so full of shame. Some love might come across his life, and purify him, and shield him from those sins that seemed to be already stirring in spirit and in flesh - those curious unpictured sins whose very mystery lent them their subtlety and their charm. Perhaps, some day, the cruel look would have passed away from the scarlet sensitive mouth, and he might show to the world Basil Hallward's masterpiece. No; that was impossible. The thing upon the canvas was growing old, hour by hour, and week by week. Even if it escaped the hideousness of sin, the hideousness of age was in store for it. The cheeks would become hollow or flaccid. Yellow crow's-feet would creep round the fading eyes and make them horrible. The hair would lose its brightness, the mouth would gape or droop, would be foolish or gross, as the mouths of old men are. There would be the wrinkled throat, the cold blue-veined hands, the twisted body, that he remembered in the uncle who had been so stern to him in his boyhood. The picture had to be concealed. There was no help for it.

"Bring it in, Mr. Ashton, please," he said, wearily, turning round. "I am sorry I kept you so long. I was thinking of something else."

"Always glad to have a rest, Mr. Gray," answered the frame-maker, who was still gasping for breath. "Where shall we put it, sir?"

"Oh, anywhere. Here, this will do. I don't want to have it hung up. Just lean it against the wall. Thanks."

"Might one look at the work of art, sir?"

Dorian started. "It would not interest you, Mr. Ashton," he said, keeping his eye on the man. He felt ready to leap upon him and fling him to the ground if he dared to lift the gorgeous hanging that concealed the secret of his life. "I won't trouble you any more now. I am much obliged for your kindness in coming round."

"Not at all, not at all, Mr. Gray. Ever ready to do anything for you, sir." And Mr. Ashton tramped down-stairs, followed by the assistant, who glanced back at Dorian with a look of shy wonder in his rough, uncomely face. He had never seen any one so marvellous.

When the sound of their footsteps had died away, Dorian locked the door, and put the key in his pocket. He felt safe now. No one would ever look on the horrible thing. No eye but his would ever see his shame.

On reaching the library he found that it was just after five o'clock, and that the tea had been already brought up. On a little table of dark perfumed wood thickly incrusted with nacre, a present from his guardian's wife, Lady Radley, who had spent the preceding winter in Cairo, was lying a note from Lord Henry, and beside it was a book bound in yellow paper, the cover slightly torn and the edges soiled. A copy of the third edition of the 'St. James's Gazette' had been placed on the tea-tray. It was evident that Victor had returned. He wondered if he had met the men in the hall as they were leaving the house and had wormed out of them what they had been doing. He would be sure to miss the picture – had no doubt missed it already, while he had been laying the tea-things. The screen had not been replaced, and the blank space on the wall was visible. Perhaps some night he might find him creeping upstairs and trying to force the door of the room. It was a horrible thing to have a spy in one's house. He had heard of rich men who had been blackmailed all their lives by some servant who had read a letter, or overheard a conversation, or picked up a card with an address, or found beneath a pillow a withered flower or a bit of crumpled lace.

He sighed, and, having poured himself out some tea, opened Lord Henry's note. It was simply to say that he sent him round the evening paper, and a book that might interest him, and that he would be at the club at eight-fifteen. He opened the 'St. James's' languidly, and looked through it. A red pencil-mark on the fifth page caught his eye. He read the following paragraph:

"INQUEST ON AN ACTRESS. – An inquest was held this morning at the Bell Tavern, Hoxton Road, by Mr. Danby, the District Coroner, on the body of Sibyl Vane, a young actress recently engaged at the Royal Theatre, Holborn. A verdict of death by misadventure was returned. Considerable sympathy was expressed for the mother of the deceased, who was greatly affected during the giving of her own evidence, and that of Dr. Birrell, who had made the postmortem examination of the deceased."

He frowned slightly, and, tearing the paper in two, went across the room and flung the pieces into a gilt basket. How ugly it all was! And how horribly real ugliness made things! He felt a little annoyed with Lord Henry for having sent him the account. And it was certainly stupid of him to have marked it with red pencil. Victor might have read it. The man knew more than enough English for that.

Perhaps he had read it, and had begun to suspect something. And, yet, what did it matter? What had Dorian Gray to do with Sibyl Vane's death? There was nothing to fear. Dorian Gray had not killed her.

His eye fell on the yellow book that Lord Henry had sent him. What was it, he wondered. He went towards the little pearl-coloured octagonal stand, that had always looked to him like the work of some strange Egyptian bees who wrought in silver, and took the volume up. He flung himself into an armchair, and began to turn over the leaves. After a few minutes, he became absorbed. It was the strangest book he had ever read. It seemed to him that in exquisite raiment, and to the delicate sound of flutes, the sins of the world were passing in dumb show before him. Things that he had dimly dreamed of were suddenly made real to him. Things of which he had never dreamed were gradually revealed.

It was a novel without a plot, and with only one character, being, indeed, simply a psychological study of a certain young Parisian, who spent his life trying to realise in the nineteenth century all the passions and modes of thought that belonged to every century except his own, and to sum up, as it were, in himself the various moods through which the world-spirit had ever passed, loving for their mere artificiality those renunciations that men have unwisely called virtue, as much as those natural rebellions that wise men still call sin. The style in which it was written was that curious jewelled style, vivid and obscure at once, full of 'argot' and of archaisms, of technical expressions and of elaborate paraphrases, that characterises the work of some of the finest artists of the French school of 'Decadents'. There were in it metaphors as monstrous as orchids, and as evil in colour. The life of the senses was described in the terms of mystical philosophy. One hardly knew at times whether one was reading the spiritual ecstasies of some mediaeval saint or the morbid confessions of a modern sinner. It was a poisonous book. The heavy odour of incense seemed to cling about its pages and to trouble the brain. The mere cadence of the sentences, the subtle monotony of their music, so full as it was of complex refrains and movements elaborately repeated, produced in the mind of the lad, as he passed from chapter to chapter, a form of revery, a malady of dreaming, that made him unconscious of the falling day and the creeping shadows.

Cloudless, and pierced by one solitary star, a copper-green sky gleamed through the windows. He read on by its wan light till he could read no more. Then, after his valet had reminded him several times of the lateness of the hour, he got up, and, going into the next room, placed the book on the little Florentine table that always stood at his bedside, and began to dress for dinner.

It was almost nine o'clock before he reached the club, where he found Lord Henry sitting alone, in the morning-room, looking very bored.

"I am so sorry, Harry," he cried, "but really it is entirely your fault. That book you sent me so fascinated me that I forgot what the time was."

"I thought you would like it," replied his host, rising from his chair.

"I didn't say I liked it, Harry. I said it fascinated me. There is a great difference."

"Ah, if you have discovered that, you have discovered a great deal," murmured Lord Henry, with his curious smile. "Come, let us go in to dinner. It is dreadfully late, and I am afraid the champagne will be too much iced."

NINE

For years, Dorian Gray could not free himself from the memory of this book. Or perhaps it would be more accurate to say that he never sought to free himself from it. He procured from Paris no less than five large-paper copies of the first edition, and had them bound in different colours, so that they might suit his various moods and the changing fancies of a nature over which he seemed, at times, to have entirely lost control. The hero, the wonderful young Parisian, in whom the romantic temperament and the scientific temperament were so strangely blended, became to him a kind of prefiguring type of himself. And, indeed, the whole book seemed to him to contain the story of his own life, written before he had lived it.

In one point he was more fortunate than the book's fantastic hero. He never knew – never, indeed, had any cause to know – that somewhat grotesque dread of mirrors, and polished metal surfaces, and still water, which came upon the young Parisian so early in his life, and was occasioned by the sudden decay of a beauty that had once, apparently, been so remarkable. It was with an almost cruel joy – and perhaps in nearly every joy, as certainly in every pleasure, cruelty had its place – that he used to read the latter part of the book, with its really tragic, if somewhat over-emphasised, account of the sorrow and despair of one who had himself lost what in others, and in the world, he had most valued.

He, at any rate, had no cause to fear that. The boyish beauty that had so fascinated Basil Hallward, and many others besides him, seemed never to leave him. Even those who had heard the most evil things against him (and from time to time strange rumours about his mode of life crept through London and became the chatter of the clubs) could not believe anything to his dishonour when they saw him. He had always the look of one who had kept himself unspotted from the world. Men who talked grossly became silent when Dorian Gray entered the room. There was something in the purity of his face that rebuked them. His mere presence seemed to recall to them the innocence that they had tarnished. They wondered how one so charming and graceful as he was could have escaped the stain of an age that was at once sordid and sensuous.

He himself, on returning home from one of those mysterious and prolonged absences that gave rise to such strange conjecture among those who were his friends, or thought that they were so, would creep upstairs to the locked room, open the door with the key that never left him, and stand, with a mirror, in front of the portrait that Basil Hallward had painted of him, looking now at the evil and aging face on the canvas, and now at the fair young face that laughed back at him from the polished glass. The very sharpness of the contrast used to quicken his sense of pleasure. He grew more and more enamoured of his own beauty, more and more interested in the corruption of his own soul. He would examine with minute care, and often with a monstrous and terrible delight, the hideous lines that seared the wrinkling forehead or crawled around the heavy sensual mouth, wondering sometimes which were the more horrible, the signs of sin or the signs of age. He would place his white hands beside the coarse and bloated hands of the picture, and smile. He mocked the misshapen body and the failing limbs.

There were moments, indeed, at night, when, lying sleepless in his own delicately-scented chamber, or in the sordid room of the little ill-famed tavern near the Docks, which, under an assumed name, and in disguise, it was his habit to frequent, he would think of the ruin he had brought upon his soul, with a pity that was all the more poignant because it was purely selfish. But moments such as these were rare. That curiosity about life that, many years before, Lord Henry had first stirred in him, as they sat together in the garden of their friend, seemed to increase with gratification. The more he knew, the more he desired to know. He had mad hungers that grew more ravenous as he fed them.

Yet he was not really reckless, at any rate in his relations to society. Once or twice every month during the winter, and on each Wednesday evening while the season lasted, he would throw open to the world his beautiful house and have the most celebrated musicians of the day to charm his guests with the wonders of their art. His little dinners, in the settling of which Lord Henry always assisted him, were noted as much for the careful selection and placing of those invited, as for the exquisite taste shown in the decoration of the table, with its subtle symphonic arrangements of exotic flowers, and embroidered cloths, and antique plate of gold and silver. Indeed, there were many, especially among the very young men, who saw, or fancied that they saw, in Dorian Gray the true realisation of a type of which they had often dreamed in Eton or Oxford days, a type that was to combine something of the real culture of the scholar with all the grace and distinction and perfect manner of a citizen of the world. To them he seemed to belong to those whom Dante describes as having sought to "make themselves perfect by the worship of beauty". Like Gautier, he was one for whom "the visible world existed".

And, certainly, to him life itself was the first, the greatest, of all arts, and for it all the other arts seemed to be but a preparation. Fashion, by which what is really fantastic becomes for a moment universal, and Dandyism, which, in its own way, is an attempt to assert the absolute modernity of beauty, had, of course, their fascination for him. His mode of dressing, and the particular styles that he affected from time to time, had their marked influence on the young exquisites of the Mayfair balls and Pall Mall club windows, who copied him in everything that he did and tried to reproduced the accidental charm of his graceful, though to him only half-serious, fopperies.

For, while he was but too ready to accept the position that was, almost immediately offered to him on his coming of age and found, indeed, a subtle pleasure in the thought that he might really become to the London of his own day what to imperial Neronian Rome the author of the 'Satyricon' had once been, yet in his inmost heart he desired to be something more than a mere 'arbiter elegantiarum', to be consulted on the wearing of a jewel, or the knotting of a necktie, or the conduct of a cane. He sought to elaborate some new scheme of life that would have its reasoned philosophy and its ordered principles and find in the spiritualising of the senses its highest realisation.

The worship of the senses has often, and with much justice, been decried, men feeling a natural instinct of terror about passions and sensations that seem stronger than ourselves, and that we are conscious of sharing with the less highly organised forms of existence. But it appeared to Dorian Gray that the true nature of the senses had never been understood, and that they had remained savage and animal merely because the world had sought to starve them into submission or to kill them by pain, instead of aiming at making them elements of a new spirituality, of which a fine instinct for beauty was to be the dominant characteristic. As he looked back upon man moving through History, he was haunted by a feeling of loss. So much had been surrendered! and to such little purpose! There had been mad wilful rejections, monstrous forms of self-torture and self-denial, whose origin was fear, and whose result was a degradation infinitely more terrible than that fancied degradation from which, in their ignorance, they had sought to escape, Nature in her wonderful irony driving the anchorite out to herd with the wild animals of the desert and giving to the hermit the beasts of the field as his companions.

Yes, there was to be, as Lord Henry had prophesied, a new hedonism that was to re-create life, and to save it from that harsh, uncomely puritanism that is having, in our own day, its curious revival. It was to have its service of the intellect, certainly; yet it was never to accept any theory or system that would involve the sacrifice of any mode of passionate experience. Its aim, indeed, was to be experience itself, and not the fruits of experience, sweet or bitter as they might be. Of the asceticism that deadens the senses, as of the vulgar profligacy that dulls them, it was to know nothing. But it was to teach man to concentrate himself upon the moments of a life that is itself but a moment.

There are few of us who have not sometimes wakened before dawn, either after one of those dreamless nights that make one almost enamoured of death, or one of those nights of horror and misshapen joy, when through the chambers of the brain sweep phantoms more terrible than reality itself, and instinct with that vivid life that lurks in all grotesques, and that lends to Gothic art its enduring vitality, this art being, one might fancy, especially the art of those whose minds have been troubled with the malady of revery. Gradually white fingers creep through the curtains, and they appear to tremble. Black fantastic shadows crawl into the corners of the room, and crouch there. Outside, there is the stirring of birds among the leaves, or the sound of men going forth to their work, or the sigh and sob of the wind coming down from the hills, and wandering round the silent house, as though it feared to wake the sleepers. Veil after veil of thin dusky gauze is lifted, and by degrees the forms and colours of things are restored to them, and we watch the dawn remaking the world in its antique pattern. The wan mirrors get back their mimic life. The flameless tapers stand where we have left them and beside them lies the half-read book that we had been studying, or the wired flower that we had worn at the ball, or the letter that we had been afraid to read, or that we had read too often. Nothing seems to us changed. Out of the unreal shadows of the night comes back the real life that we had known. We have to resume it where we had left off, and there steals over us a terrible sense of the necessity for the continuance of energy in the same wearisome round of stereotyped habits, or a wild longing, it may be, that our eyelids might open some morning upon a world that had been re-fashioned anew for our pleasure in the darkness, a world in which things would have fresh shapes and colours, and be changed, or have other secrets, a world in which the past would have little or no place, or survive, at any rate, in no conscious form of obligation or regret, the remembrance of joy having its bitterness, and the memories of pleasure, their pain.

It was the creation of such worlds as these that seemed to Dorian Gray to be the true object, or among the true objects, of life; and in his search for sensations that would be at once new and delightful, and possess that element of strangeness that is so essential to romance, he would often adopt certain modes of thought that he knew to be really alien to his nature, abandon himself to their subtle influences, and then, having, as it were, caught their colour and satisfied his intellectual curiosity, leave them with that curious indifference that is not compatible with a real ardour of temperament, and that indeed, according to certain modern psychologists, is often a condition of it.

It was rumoured of him once that he was about to join the Roman Catholic communion; and certainly the Roman ritual had always a great attraction for him. The daily sacrifice, more awful really than all the sacrifices of the antique world, stirred him as much by its superb rejection of the evidence of the senses as by the primitive simplicity of its elements and the eternal pathos of the human tragedy that it sought to symbolise. He loved to kneel down on the cold marble pavement, and with the priest, in his stiff flowered cope, slowly and with white hands moving aside the veil of the tabernacle, and raising aloft the jewelled lantern-shaped monstrance with that pallid wafer that at times, one would fain think, is indeed the 'panis caelestis', the bread of angels, or, robed in the garments of the Passion of Christ, breaking the Host into the chalice, and smiting his breast for his sins. The fuming censers, that the grave boys, in their lace and scarlet, tossed into the air like great gilt flowers, had their subtle fascination for him. As he passed out, he used to look with wonder at the black confessionals, and long to sit in the dim shadow of one of them and listen to men and women whispering through the tarnished grating the true story of their lives.

But he never fell into the error of arresting his intellectual development by any formal acceptance of creed or system, or of mistaking, for a house in which to live, an inn that is but suitable for the sojourn of a night, or for a few hours of a night in which there are no stars and the moon is in travail. Mysticism, with its marvellous power of making common things strange to us, and the subtle antinomianism that always seems to accompany it, moved him for a season; and for a season he inclined to the materialistic doctrines of the 'Darwinismus' movement in Germany, and found a curious pleasure in tracing the thoughts and passions of men to some pearly cell in the brain, or some white nerve in the body, delighting in the conception of the absolute dependence of the spirit on certain physical conditions, morbid or healthy, normal or diseased. Yet, as has been said of him before, no theory of life seemed to him to be of any importance compared with life itself. He felt keenly conscious of how barren all intellectual speculation is, when separated from action and experiment. He knew that the senses, no less than the soul, have their mysteries to reveal.

And so he would now study perfumes, and the secrets of

their manufacture, distilling heavily-scented oils, and burning odorous gums from the East. He saw that there was no mood of the mind that had not its counterpart in the sensuous life, and set himself to discover their true relations, wondering what there was in frankincense that made one mystical, and in ambergris that stirred one's passions, and in violets that woke the memory of dead romances, and in musk that troubled the brain, and in champak that stained the imagination; and seeking often to elaborate a real psychology of perfumes, and to estimate the several influences of sweet-smelling roots, and scented pollen-laden flowers, of aromatic balms, and of dark and fragrant woods, of spikenard that sickens, of hovenia that makes men mad, and of aloes that are said to be able to expel melancholy from the soul.

At another time he devoted himself entirely to music, and in a long latticed room, with a vermilion-and-gold ceiling and walls of olive-green lacquer, he used to give curious concerts in which mad gypsies tore wild music from little zithers, or grave yellow shawled Tunisians plucked at the strained strings or monstrous lutes, while grinning negroes beat monotonously upon copper drums, or turbaned Indians, crouching upon scarlet mats, blew through long pipes of reed or brass, and charmed, or feigned to charm, great hooded snakes and horrible horned adders. The harsh intervals and shrill discords of barbaric music stirred him at times when Schubert's grace, and Chopin's beautiful sorrows, and the mighty harmonies of Beethoven himself, fell unheeded on his ear. He collected together from all parts of the world the strangest instruments that could be found, either in the tombs of dead nations or among the few savage tribes that have survived contact with Western civilisations, and loved to touch and try them. He had the mysterious 'juruparis' of the Rio Negro Indians, that women are not allowed to look at, and that even youths may not see till they have been subjected to fasting and scourging, and the earthen jars of the Peruvians that have the shrill cries of birds, and flutes of human bones such as Alfonso de Ovalle heard in Chile, and the sonorous green stones that are found near Cuzco and give forth a note of singular sweetness. He had painted gourds filled with pebbles that rattled when they were shaken; the long 'clarin' of the Mexicans, into which the performer does not blow, but through which he inhales the air; the harsh 'ture' of the Amazon tribes, that is sounded by the sentinels who sit all day long in trees, and that can be heard, it is said, at a distance of three leagues; the 'teponaztli', that has two vibrating tongues of wood, and is beaten with sticks that are smeared with an elastic gum obtained from the milky juice of plants; the 'yotl' bells of the Aztecs, that are hung in clusters like grapes; and a huge cylindrical drum, covered with the skins of great serpents, like the one that Bernal Diaz saw when he went with Cortes into the Mexican temple, and of whose doleful sound he has left us so vivid a description. The fantastic character of these instruments fascinated him, and he felt a curious delight in the thought that Art, like Nature, has her monsters, things of bestial shape and with hideous voices. Yet, after some time he wearied of them, and would sit in his box at the Opera, either alone or with Lord Henry listening in rapt pleasure to 'Tannhäuser', and seeing in the great work of art a presentation of the tragedy of his own soul.

On another occasion he took up the study of jewels, and appeared at a costume ball as Anne de Joyeuse, Admiral of France, in a dress covered with five hundred and sixty pearls. He would often spend a whole day settling and resettling in their cases the various stones that he had collected, such as the olive-green chrysoberyl that turns red by lamplight, the cymophane with its wire-like line of silver, the pistachio-coloured peridot, rose-pink and wine-yellow topazes, carbuncles of fiery scarlet with tremulous four-rayed stars, flame-red cinnamon-stones, orange and violet spinels, and amethysts with their alternate layers of ruby and sapphire. He loved the red gold of the sunstone, and the moonstone's pearly whiteness, and the broken rainbow of the milky opal. He procured from Amsterdam three emeralds of extraordinary size and richness of colour, and had a turquoise 'de la vieille roche' that was the envy of all the connoisseurs.

He discovered wonderful stories, also, about jewels. In Alphonso's 'Clericalis Disciplina' a serpent was mentioned with eyes of real jacinth, and in the romantic history of Alexander he was said to have found snakes in the vale of Jordan "with collars of real emeralds growing on their backs". There was a gem in the brain of the dragon, Philostratus told us, and "by the exhibition of golden letters and a scarlet robe" the monster could be thrown into a magical sleep, and slain. According to the great alchemist Pierre de Boniface, the diamond rendered a man invisible, and the agate of India made him eloquent. The cornelian appeased anger, and the hyacinth provoked sleep, and the amethyst drove away the fumes of wine. The garnet cast out demons, and the hydropicus deprived the moon of her colour. The selenite waxed and waned with the moon, and the meloceus, that discovers thieves, could be affected only by the blood of kids. Leonardus Camillus had seen a white stone taken from the brain of a newly-killed toad, that was a certain antidote against poison. The bezoar, that was found in the heart of the Arabian deer, was a charm that could cure the plague. In the nests of Arabian birds was the aspirates, that, according to Democritus, kept the wearer from any danger by fire.

The King of Ceilan rode through his city with a large ruby in his hand, as the ceremony of his coronation. The gates of the palace of John the Priest were "made of sardius, with the horn of the horned snake inwrought, so that no man might bring poison within". Over the gable were "two golden apples, in which were two carbuncles", so that the gold might shine by day, and the carbuncles by night. In Lodge's strange romance 'A Margarite of America' it was stated that in the chamber of Margarite were seen "all the chaste ladies of the world, inchased out of silver, looking through fair mirrors of chrysolites, carbuncles, sapphires, and greene emeraults". Marco Polo had watched the inhabitants of Zipangu place a rose-coloured pearl in the mouth of the dead. A sea-monster had been enamoured of the pearl that the diver brought to King Perozes, and had slain the thief, and mourned for seven moons over his loss. When the Huns lured the king into the great pit, he flung it away – Procopius tells the story – nor was it ever found again, though the Emperor Anastasius offered five hundred weight of gold pieces for it. The King of Malabar had shown a Venetian a rosary of one hundred and four pearls, one for every god that he worshipped.

When the Duke de Valentinois, son of Alexander VI, visited Louis XII of France, his horse was loaded with gold leaves, according to Brantome, and his cap had double rows of rubies that threw out a great light. Charles of England had ridden in stirrups hung with three hundred and twenty-one diamonds. Richard II had a coat, valued at thirty thousand marks, which was covered with balus rubies. Hall described Henry VIII, on his way to the Tower previous to his coronation, as wearing "a jacket of raised gold, the placard embroidered with diamonds and other rich stones, and a great bauderike about his neck of large balasses". The favourites of James I wore ear-rings of emeralds set in gold filigrane. Edward II gave to Piers Gaveston a suit of red-gold armour studded with jacinths, and a collar of gold roses set with turquoise-stones, and a skullcap parsemé with pearls. Henry II wore jewelled gloves reaching to the elbow, and had a hawk-glove set with twelve rubies and fifty-two great pearls. The ducal hat of Charles the Rash, the last Duke of Burgundy of his race, was studded with sapphires and hung with pear-shaped pearls.

How exquisite life had once been! How gorgeous in its pomp and decoration! Even to read of the luxury of the dead was wonderful.

Then he turned his attention to embroideries, and to the tapestries that performed the office of frescoes in the chill rooms of the Northern nations of Europe. As he investigated the subject – and he always had an extraordinary faculty of becoming absolutely absorbed for the moment in whatever he took up – he was almost saddened by the reflection of the ruin that time brought on beautiful and wonderful things. He, at any rate, had escaped that. Summer followed summer, and the yellow jonquils bloomed and died many times, and nights of horror repeated the story of their shame, but he was unchanged. No winter marred his face or stained his flower-like bloom. How different it was with material things! Where had they gone to? Where was the great crocus-coloured robe, on which the gods fought against the giants, that had been worked for Athena? Where the huge velarium that Nero had stretched across the Colosseum at Rome, on which were represented the starry sky, and Apollo driving a chariot drawn by white gilt-reined steeds? He longed to see the curious table-napkins wrought for Elagabalus, on which were displayed all the dainties and viands that could be wanted for a feast; the mortuary cloth of King Chilperic, with its three hundred golden bees; the fantastic robes that excited the indignation of the Bishop of Pontus, and were figured with "lions, panthers, bears, dogs, forests, rocks, hunters – all, in fact, that a painter can copy from nature"; and the coat that Charles of Orléans once wore, on the sleeves of which were embroidered the verses of a song beginning "Madame, je suis tout joyeux", the musical accompaniment of the words being wrought in gold thread, and each note, a square shape in those days, formed with four pearls. He read of the room that was prepared at the palace at Rheims for the use of Queen Joan of Burgundy, and was decorated with "thirteen hundred and twenty-one parrots, made in broidery, and blazoned with the king's arms, and five hundred and sixty-one butterflies, whose wings were similarly ornamented with the arms of the queen, the whole worked in gold". Catherine de Medicis had a mourning-bed made for her of black velvet powdered with crescents and suns. Its curtains were of damask, with leafy wreaths and garlands, figured upon a gold and silver ground, and fringed along the edges with broideries of pearls, and it stood in a room hung with rows of the queen's devices in cut black velvet upon cloth of silver. Louis XIV had gold-embroidered caryatides fifteen feet high in his apartment. The state bed of Sobeiski, King of Poland, was made of Smyrna gold brocade embroidered in turquoises with verses from the Koran. Its supports were of silver gilt, beautifully chased, and profusely set with enamelled and jewelled medallions. It had been taken from the Turkish camp before Vienna, and the standard of Mohammed had stood under it.

And so, for a whole year, he sought to accumulate the most exquisite specimens that he could find of textile and embroidered work, getting the dainty Delhi muslins, finely wrought, with gold-thread palmates, and stitched over with iridescent beetles' wings; the Dacca gauzes, that from their transparency are known in the East as 'woven air', and 'running water', and 'evening dew'; strange figured cloths from Java; elaborate yellow Chinese hangings; books bound in tawny satins or fair blue silks and wrought with fleurs de lys, birds, and images; veils of 'lacis' worked in Hungary point; Sicilian brocades and stiff Spanish velvets; Georgian work with its gilt coins, and Japanese 'Foukousas' with their green-toned golds and their marvellously plumaged birds.

He had a special passion, also, for ecclesiastical vestments, as indeed he had for everything connected with the service of the Church. In the long cedar chests that lined the west gallery of his house he had stored away many rare and beautiful specimens of what is really the raiment of the Bride of Christ, who must wear purple and jewels and fine linen that she may hide the palled macerated body that is worn by the suffering that she seeks for, and wounded by self-inflicted pain. He had a gorgeous cope of crimson silk and gold-thread damask, figured with a repeating pattern of golden pomegranates set in six-petalled formal blossoms, beyond which on either side was the pine-apple device wrought in seed-pearls. The orphreys were divided into panels representing scenes from the life of the Virgin, and the coronation of the Virgin was figured in coloured silks upon the hood. This was Italian work of the fifteenth century. Another copy was of green velvet, embroidered with heart-shaped groups of acanthus-leaves, from which spread long-stemmed white blossoms, the details of which were picked out with silver thread and coloured crystals. The morse bore a seraph's head in gold-thread raised work. The orphreys were woven in a diaper of red and gold silk, and were starred with medallions of many saints and martyrs, among whom was St. Sebastian. He had chasubles, also, of amber-coloured silk, and blue silk and gold brocade, and yellow silk damask and cloth of gold, figured with representations of the Passion and Crucifixion of Christ, and embroidered with lions and peacocks and other emblems; dalmatics of white satin and pink silk damask, decorated with tulips and dolphins and fleurs de lys; altar frontals of crimson velvet and blue linen; and many corporals, chalice-veils, and sudaria. In the mystic offices to which these things were put there was something that quickened his imagination.

For these things, and everything that he collected in his lovely house, were to be to him means for forgetfulness, modes by which he could escape, for a season, from the fear that seemed to him at times to be almost too great to be borne. Upon the walls of the lonely locked room where he had spent so much of his boyhood, he had hung with his own hands the terrible portrait whose changing features showed him the real degradation of his life, and had draped the purple-and-gold pall in front of it as a curtain. For weeks he would not go there, would forget the hideous painted thing, and get back his light heart, his wonderful joyousness, his passionate pleasure in mere existence. Then, suddenly, some night he would creep out of the house, go down to dreadful places near Blue Gate Fields, and stay there, day after day, until he was driven away. On his return he would sit in front of the picture, sometimes loathing it and himself, but filled, at other times, with that pride of rebellion that is half the fascination of sin, and smiling, with secret pleasure, at the misshapen shadow that had to bear the burden that should have been his own.

After a few years he could not endure to be long out of England, and gave up the villa that he had shared at Trouville with Lord Henry, as well as the little white walled-in house at Algiers where he had more than once spent his winter. He hated to be separated from the picture that was such a part of his life, and he was also afraid that during his absence some one might gain access to the room, in spite of the elaborate bolts and bars that he had caused to be placed upon the door.

He was quite conscious that this would tell them nothing. It is true that the portrait still preserved, under all the foulness and ugliness of the face, its marked likeness to himself; but what could they learn from that? He would laugh at any one who tried to taunt him. He had not painted it. What was it to him how vile and full of shame it looked? Even if he told them, would they believe it?

Yet he was afraid. Sometimes when he was down at his great house in Nottinghamshire, entertaining the fashionable young men of his own rank who were his chief companions, and astounding the county by the wanton luxury and gorgeous splendour of his mode of life, he would suddenly leave his guests and rush back to town to see that the door had not been tampered with and that the picture was still there. What if it should be stolen? The mere thought made him cold with horror. Surely the world would know his secret then. Perhaps the world already suspected it.

For, while he fascinated many, there were not a few who distrusted him. He was blackballed at a West End club of which his birth and social position fully entitled him to become a member, and on one occasion, when he was brought by a friend into the smoking-room of the Carlton, the Duke of Berwick and another gentleman got up in a marked manner and went out. Curious stories became current about him after he had passed his twenty-fifth year. It was said that he had been seen brawling with foreign sailors in a low den in the distant part of Whitechapel, and that he consorted with thieves and coiners and knew the mysteries of their trade. His extraordinary absences became notorious, and, when he used to reappear again in society, men would whisper to each other in corners, or pass him with a sneer, or look at him with cold searching eyes, as if they were determined to discover his secret.

Of such insolences and attempted slights he, of course, took no notice, and in the opinion of most people his frank debonair manner, his charming boyish smile, and the infinite grace of that wonderful youth that seemed never to leave him, were in themselves a sufficient answer to the calumnies (for so they called them) that were circulated about him. It was remarked, however, that those who had been most intimate with him appeared, after a time, to shun him. Of all his friends, or so-called friends, Lord Henry Wotton was the only one who remained loyal to him. Women who had wildly adored him, and for his sake had braved all social censure and set convention at defiance, were seen to grow pallid with shame or horror if Dorian Gray entered the room.

Yet these whispered scandals only lent him, in the eyes of many, his strange and dangerous charm. His great wealth was a certain element of security. Society, civilised society at least, is never very ready to believe anything to the detriment of those who are both rich and charming. It feels instinctively that manners are of more importance than morals, and the highest respectability is of less value in its opinion that the possession of a good chef. And, after all, it is a very poor consolation to be told that the man who has given one a bad dinner, or poor wine, is irreproachable in his private life. Even the cardinal virtues cannot atone for cold entrées, as Lord Henry remarked once, in a discussion on the subject; and there is possibly a good deal to be said for his view. For the canons of good society are, or should be, the same as the canons of art. Form is absolutely essential to it. It should have the dignity of a ceremony, as well as its unreality, and should combine the insincere character of a romantic play with the wit and beauty that make such plays charming. Is insincerity such a terrible thing? I think not. It is merely a method by which we can multiply our personalities.

Such, at any rate, was Dorian Gray's opinion. He used to wonder at the shallow psychology of those who conceive the Ego in man as a thing simple, permanent, reliable, and of one essence. To him, man was a being with myriad lives and myriad sensations, a complex-multi-form creature that bore within itself strange legacies of thought and passion, and whose very flesh was tainted with the monstrous maladies of the dead. He loved to stroll through the gaunt cold picture-gallery of his country-house and look at the various portraits of those whose blood flowed in his veins. Here was Philip Herbert, described by Francis Osborne, in his 'Memories on the Reigns of Queen Elizabeth and King James', as one who was "caressed by the court for his handsome face which kept him not long company". Was it young Herbert's life that he sometimes led? Had some strange poisonous germ crept from body to body till it had reached his own? Was it some dim sense of that ruined grace that had made him so suddenly, and almost without cause, give utterance, in Basil Hallward's studio, to that mad prayer that had so changed his life? Here, in gold-embroidered red doublet, jewelled surcoat, and gilt-edged ruff and wrist-bands, stood Sir Anthony Sherard, with his silver-and-black armour piled at his feet. What had this man's legacy been? Had the lover of Giovanna of Naples bequeathed him some inheritance of sin and shame? Were his own actions merely the dreams that the dead man had not dared to realise? Here, from the fading canvas, smiled Lady Elizabeth Devereux, in her gauze hood, pearl stomacher, and pink slashed sleeves. A flower was in her right hand, and her left clasped an enamelled collar of white and damask roses. On a table by her side lay a mandolin and an apple. There were large green rosettes upon her little pointed shoes. He knew her life, and the strange stories that were told about her lovers. Had he something of her temperament in him? Those oval heavy-lidded eyes seemed to look curiously at him. What of George Willoughby, with his powdered hair and fantastic patches? How evil he looked! The face was saturnine and swarthy, and the sensual lips seemed to be twisted with disdain. Delicate lace ruffles fell over the lean yellow hands that were so overladen with rings. He had been a Macaroni of the eighteenth century, and the friend, in his youth, of Lord Ferrars. What of the second Lord Sherard, the companion of the Prince Regent in his wildest days, and one of the witnesses at the secret marriage with Mrs. Fitzherbert? How proud and handsome he was, with his chestnut curls and insolent pose! What passions had he bequeathed? The world had looked upon him as infamous. He had led the orgies at Carlton House. The star of the Garter glittered upon his breast. Beside him hung the portrait of his wife, a pallid, thin-lipped woman in black. Her blood, also, stirred within him. How curious it all seemed!

Yet one had ancestors in literature, as well as in one's own race, nearer perhaps in type and temperament, many of them, and certainly with an influence of which one was more absolutely conscious. There were times when it seemed to Dorian Gray that the whole of history was merely the record of his own life, not as he had lived it in act and circumstances, but as his imagination had created it for him, as it had been in his brain and in his passions. He felt that he had known them all, those strange terrible figures that he had passed across the stage of the world and made sin so marvellous and evil so full of wonder. It seemed to him that in some mysterious way their lives had been his own.

The hero of the dangerous novel that had so influenced his life had himself had this curious fancy. In a chapter of the book he tells how, crowned with a laurel, lest lightning might strike him, he had sat, as Tiberius, in a garden at Capri, reading the shameful books of Elephantis, while dwarfs and peacocks strutted round him and the flute-player mocked the swinger of the censer; and, as Caligula, had caroused with the green-shined jockeys in their stables, and supped in an ivory manger with a jewel-frontletted horse; and, as Domitian, had wandered through a corridor lined with marble mirrors, looking round with haggard eyes for the reflection of the dagger that was to end his days, and sick with that ennui, that 'taedium vitae', that comes on those to whom life denies nothing; and had peered through a clear emerald at the red shambles of the Circus, and then, in a litter of pearl and purple drawn by silver-shod mules, been carried through the Street of Pomegranates to a House of Gold, and heard men cry on Nero 'Caesar' as he passed by; and, as Elagabalus, had painted his face with colours, and plied the distaff among the women, and brought the Moon from Carthage, and given her in mystic marriage to the Sun.

Over and over again Dorian used to read this fantastic chapter, and the chapter immediately following, in which the hero describes the curious tapestries that he had had woven for him from Gustave Moreau's designs, and on which were pictured the awful and beautiful forms of those whom Vice and Blood and Weariness had made monstrous or mad. Filipo, Duke of Milan, who slew his wife, and painted her lips with a scarlet poison; Pietro Barbi, the Venetian, known as Paul the Second, who sought in his vanity to assume the title of Formosus, and whose tiara, valued at two hundred thousand florins, was bought at the price of a terrible sin; Gian Maria Visconti, who used hounds to chase living men, and whose murdered body was covered with roses by a harlot who had loved him; the Borgia on his white horse, with Fratricide riding beside him, and his mantle stained with the blood of Perotto; Pietro Riario, the young Cardinal Archbishop of Florence, child and minion of Sixtus IV, whose beauty was equalled only by his debauchery, and who received Leonora of Aragon in a pavilion of white and crimson silk, filled with nymphs and centaurs, and gilded a boy that he might serve her at the feast as Ganymede or Hylas; Ezzelin, whose melancholy could be cured only by the spectacle of death, and who had a passion for red blood, as other men have for red wine – the son of the Fiend, as was reported, and one who had cheated his father at dice when gambling with him for his own soul; Giambattista Cibo, who in mockery took the name of Innocent, and into whose torpid veins the blood of three lads was infused by a Jewish doctor; Sigismondo Malatesta, the lover of Isotta, and the lord of Rimini, whose effigy was burned at Rome as the enemy of God and man, who strangled Polyssena with a napkin, and gave poison to Ginerva d'Este in a cup of emerald, and in honour of a shameful passion built a pagan church for Christian worship; Charles VI, who had so wildly adored his brother's wife that a leper had warned him of the insanity that was coming on him, and who could only be soothed by Saracen cards painted with the images of Love and Death and Madness; and, in his trimmed jerkin and jewelled cap and acanthus-like curls, Grifonetto Baglioni, who slew Astorre with his bride, and Simonetto with his page, and whose comeliness was such that, as he lay dying in the yellow piazza of Perugia, those who had hated him could not choose but weep, and Atalanta, who had cursed him, blessed him.

There was a horrible fascination in them all. He saw them at night and they troubled his imagination in the day. The Renaissance knew of strange manners of poisoning – poisoning by a helmet and a lighted torch, by an embroidered glove and a jewelled fan, by a gilded pomander and by an amber chain. Dorian Gray had been poisoned by a book. There were moments when he looked on evil simply as a mode through which he could realise his conception of the beautiful.

TEN

It was on the 7th of November, the eve of his own thirty-second birthday, as he often remembered afterwards.

He was walking home about eleven o'clock from Lord Henry's, where he had been dining, and was wrapped in heavy furs, as the night was cold and foggy. At the corner of Grosvenor Square and South Audley Street a man passed him in the mist, walking very fast, and with the collar of his grey ulster turned up. He had a bag in his hand. He recognized him. It was Basil Hallward. A strange sense of fear, for which he could not account, came over him. He made no sign of recognition, and went on slowly, in the direction of his own house.

But Hallward had seen him. Dorian heard him first stopping, and then hurrying after him. In a few moments his hand was on his arm.

"Dorian! What an extraordinary piece of luck! I have been waiting for you ever since nine o'clock in your library. Finally I took pity on your tired servant, and told him to go to bed, as he let me out. I am off to Paris by the midnight train, and I wanted particularly to see you before I left. I thought it was you, or rather your fur coat, as you passed me. But I wasn't quite sure. Didn't you recognise me?"

"In this fog, my dear Basil? Why, I can't even recognise

Grosvenor Square. I believe my house is somewhere about here, but I don't feel at all certain about it. I am sorry you are going away, as I have not seen you for ages. But I suppose you will be back soon?"

"No: I am going to be out of England for six months. I intend to take a studio in Paris, and shut myself up till I have finished a great picture I have in my head. However, it wasn't about myself I wanted to talk. Here we are at your door. Let me come in for a moment. I have something to say to you."

"I shall be charmed. But won't you miss your train?" said Dorian Gray, languidly, as he passed up the steps and opened the door with his latch-key.

The lamp-light struggled out through the fog, and Hallward looked at his watch. "I have heaps of time," he answered. "The train doesn't go till twelve-fifteen, and it is only just eleven. In fact, I was on my way to the club to look for you, when I met you. You see, I shan't have any delay about luggage, as I have sent on my heavy things. All I have with me is in this bag, and I can easily get to Victoria in twenty minutes."

Dorian looked at him and smiled. "What a way for a fashionable painter to travel! A Gladstone bag, and an ulster! Come in, or the fog will get into the house. And mind you don't talk about anything serious. Nothing is serious nowadays. At least nothing should be."

Hallward shook his head, as he entered, and followed Dorian into the library. There was a bright wood fire blazing in the large open hearth. The lamps were lit, and an open Dutch silver spirit-case stood, with some siphons of soda-water and large cut-glass tumblers, on a little table.

"You see your servant made me quite at home, Dorian. He gave me everything I wanted, including your best cigarettes. He is a most hospitable creature. I like him much better than the Frenchman you used to have. What has become of the Frenchman, by the bye?"

Dorian shrugged his shoulders. "I believe he married Lady Ashton's maid, and has established her in Paris as an English dressmaker. 'Anglomanie' is very fashionable over there now, I hear. It seems silly of the French, doesn't it? But – do you know? – he was not at all a bad servant. I never liked him, but I had nothing to complain about. One often imagines things that are quite absurd. He was really very devoted to me, and seemed quite sorry when he went away. Have another brandy-and-soda? Or would you like hock-and-seltzer? I always take hock-and-seltzer myself. There is sure to be some in the next room."

"Thanks, I won't have anything more," said Hallward, taking his cap and coat off, and throwing them on the bag that he had placed in the corner. "And now, my dear fellow, I want to speak to you seriously. Don't frown like that. You make it so much more difficult for me."

"What is it all about?" cried Dorian, in his petulant way, flinging himself down on the sofa. "I hope it is not about myself. I am tired of myself to-night. I should like to be somebody else."

"It is about yourself," answered Hallward, in his grave, deep voice, "and I must say it to you. I shall only keep you half an hour."

Dorian sighed, and lit a cigarette. "Half an hour!" he murmured.

"It is not much to ask of you, Dorian, and it is entirely for your own sake that I am speaking. I think it right that you should know that the most dreadful things are being said about you in London – things that I could hardly repeat to you."

"I don't wish to know anything about them. I love scandals about other people, but scandals about myself don't interest me. They have not got the charm of novelty."

"They must interest you, Dorian. Every gentleman is interested in his good name. You don't want people to talk of you as something vile and degraded. Of course you have your position, and your wealth, and all that kind of thing. But position and wealth are not everything. Mind you, I don't believe these rumours at all. At least, I can't believe them when I see you. Sin is a thing that writes itself across a man's face. It cannot be concealed. People talk of secret vices. There are no such things as secret vices. If a wretched man has a vice, it shows itself in the lines of his mouth, the droop of his eyelids, the moulding of his hands even. Somebody – I won't mention his name, but you know him – came to me last year to have his portrait done. I had never seen him before and had never heard anything about him at the time, though I have heard a good deal since. He offered an extravagant price. I refused him. There was something in the shape of his fingers that I hated. I know now that I was quite right in what I fancied about him. His life is dreadful. But you, Dorian, with your pure, bright, innocent face, and your marvellous untroubled youth – I can't believe anything against you. And yet I see you very seldom, and you never come down to the studio now, and when I am away from you, and I hear all these hideous things that people are whispering about you, I don't know what to say. Why is it, Dorian, that a man like the Duke of Berwick leaves the room of a club when you enter it? Why is it that so many gentlemen in London will neither go to your house nor invite you to theirs? You used to be a friend of Lord Cawdor. I met him at dinner last week. Your name happened to come up in conversation, in connection with the miniatures you have lent to the exhibition at the Dudley. Cawdor curled his lip, and said that you might have the most artistic tastes, but that you were a man whom no pure-minded girl should be allowed to know, and whom no chaste woman should sit in the same room with. I remind him that I was a friend of yours, and asked him what he meant. He told me. He told me right out before everybody. It was horrible! Why is your friendship so fateful to young men? There was that wretched boy in the Guards who committed suicide. You were his great friend. There was Sir Henry Ashton, who had to leave England, with a tarnished name. You and he were inseparable. What about Adrian Singleton, and his dreadful end? What about Lord Kent's only son, and his career? I met his father yesterday in St. James Street. He seemed broken with shame and sorrow. What about the young Duke of Perth? What sort of life has he got now? What gentleman would associate with him? Dorian, Dorian, your reputation is infamous. I know you and Harry are great friends. I say nothing about that now, but surely you need not have made his sister's name a by-word. When you met Lady Gwendolen, not a breath of scandal had ever touched her. Is there a single decent woman in London now who would drive with her in the Park? Why, even her children are not allowed to live with her. Then there are other stories – stories that you have been seen creeping at dawn out of dreadful houses and slinking in disguise into the foulest dens in London. Are they true? Can they be true? When I first heard them, I laughed. I hear them now, and they make me shudder. What about your country-house, and the life that is led there? Dorian, you don't know what is said about you. I won't tell you that I don't want to preach to you. I remember Harry saying once that every man who turned himself into an amateur curate for the moment always said that, and then broke his word. I do want to preach to you. I want you to lead such a life as will make the world respect you. I want you to have a clean name and a fair record. I want you to get rid of the dreadful people you associate with. Don't shrug your shoulders like that. Don't be so indifferent. You have a wonderful influence. Let it be for good, not evil. They say that you corrupt every one whom you become intimate with, and that it is quite sufficient for you to enter a house, for shame of some kind to follow after you. I don't know whether it is so or not. How should I know? But it is said of you. I am told things that it seems impossible to doubt. Lord Gloucester was one of my greatest friends at Oxford. He showed me a letter that his wife had written to him when she was dying alone in her villa at Mentone. Your name was implicated in the most terrible confession I ever read. I told him that it was absurd – that I knew you thoroughly, and that you were incapable of anything of that kind. Know you? I wonder do I know you? Before I could answer that, I should have to see your soul."

"To see my soul!" muttered Dorian Gray, starting up from the sofa and turning almost white from fear.

"Yes," answered Hallward, gravely, and with infinite sorrow in his voice – "to see your soul. But only God can do that."

A bitter laugh of mockery broke from the lips of the younger man. "You shall see it yourself, tonight!" he cried, seizing a lamp from the table. "Come: it is your own handiwork. Why shouldn't you look at it? You can tell the world all about it afterwards, if you choose. Nobody would believe you. If they did believe you, they'd like me all the better for it. I know the age better than you do, though you will prate about it so tediously. Come, I tell you. You have chattered enough about corruption. Now you shall look on it face to face."

There was the madness of pride in every word he uttered. He stamped his foot upon the ground in his boyish insolent manner. He felt a terrible joy at the thought that some one else was to share his secret, and that the man who had painted the portrait that was the origin of all his shame was to be burdened for the rest of his life with the hideous memory of what he had done.

"Yes," he continued, coming closer to him, and looking steadfastly into his stern eyes, "I will show you my soul. You shall see the thing that you fancy only God can see."

Hallward started back. "This is blasphemy, Dorian!" he cried. "You must not say things like that. They are horrible, and they don't mean anything."

"You thing so?" He laughed again.

"I know so. As for what I said to you to-night, I said it for your good. You know I have been always devoted to you."

"Don't touch me. Finish what you have to say."

A twisted flash of pain shot across Hallward's face. He

paused for a moment, and a wild feeling of pity came over him. After all, what right had he to pry into the life of Dorian Gray? If he had done a tithe of what was rumoured about him, how much he must have suffered! Then he straightened himself up, and walked over to the fireplace, and stood there, looking at the burning logs with their frost-like ashes and their throbbing cores of flame.

"I am waiting, Basil," said the young man, in a hard, clear voice.

He turned round. "What I have to say is this," he cried. "You must give me some answer to these horrible charges that are made against you. If you tell me that they are absolutely untrue from beginning to end, I will believe you. Deny them, Dorian, deny them! Can't you see what I am going through? My God! don't tell me that you are infamous!"

Dorian Gray smiled. There was a curl of contempt in his lips. "Come up-stairs, Basil," he said quietly. "I keep a diary of my life from day to day, and it never leaves the room in which it is written. I will show you if you come with me."

"I will come with you, Dorian, if you wish it. I see I have missed my train. That makes no matter. I can go to-morrow. But don't ask me to read any thing to-night. All I want is a plain answer to my question."

"That will be given to you up-stairs. I could not give it here. You won't have to read long. Don't keep me waiting."

ELEVEN

He passed out of the room, and began the ascent, Basil Hallward following close behind. They walked softly, as men instinctively do at night. The lamp cast fantastic shadows on the wall and staircase. A rising wind made some of the windows rattle.

When they reached the top landing, Dorian set the lamp down on the floor, and taking out the key turned it in the lock. "You insist on knowing, Basil?" he asked, in a low voice.

"Yes."

"I am delighted," he murmured, smiling. Then he added, somewhat bitterly, "You are the one man in the world who is entitled to know everything about me. You have had more to do with my life than you think." And, taking up the lamp, he opened the door and went in. A cold current of air passed them, and the light shot up for a moment in a flame of murky orange. He shuddered. "Shut the door behind you," he said, as he placed the lamp on the table.

Hallward glanced round him, with a puzzled expression. The room looked as if it had not been lived in for years. A faded Flemish tapestry, a curtained picture, an old Italian 'cassone', and an almost empty bookcase – that was all it seemed to contain, besides a chair and a table. As Dorian Gray was lighting a half-burned candle that was standing on the mantel-shelf, he saw that the whole place was covered with dust, and that the carpet was in holes. A mouse ran scuffling behind the wainscoting. There was a damp odour of mildew.

"So you think that it is only God who sees the soul, Basil? Draw that curtain back, and you will see mine."

The voice that spoke was cold and cruel. "You are mad, Dorian, or playing a part," muttered Hallward, frowning.

"You won't? Then I must do it myself," said the young man; and he tore the curtain from its rod, and flung it on the ground.

An exclamation of horror broke from Hallward's lips as he saw in the dim light the hideous thing on the canvas leering at him. There was something in its expression that filled him with disgust and loathing. Good heavens! it was Dorian Gray's own face that he was looking at! The horror, whatever it was, had not yet entirely marred that marvellous beauty. There was still some gold in the thinning hair and some scarlet on the sensual lips. The sodden eyes had kept something of the loveliness of their blue, the noble curves had not yet passed entirely away from chiselled nostrils and from plastic throat. Yes, it was Dorian himself. But who had done it? He seemed to recognise his own brushwork, and the frame was his own design. The idea was monstrous, yet he felt afraid. He seized the lighted candle, and held it to the picture. In the left-hand corner was his own name, traced in long letters of bright vermilion.

It was some foul parody, some infamous, ignoble satire. He had never done that. Still, it was his own picture. He knew it, and felt as if his blood had changed from fire to sluggish ice in a moment. His own picture! What did it mean? Why had it altered? He turned, and looked at Dorian Gray with the eyes of a sick man. His mouth twitched, and his parched tongue seemed unable to articulate. He passed his hand across his forehead. It was dank with clammy sweat.

The young man was leaning against the mantelshelf, watching him with that strange expression that is on the faces of those who are absorbed in a play when a great artist is acting. There was neither real sorrow in it nor real joy. There was simply the passion of the spectator, with perhaps a flicker of triumph in the eyes. He had taken the flower out of his coat, and was smelling it, or pretending to do so.

"What does this mean?" cried Hallward, at last. His own voice sounded shrill and curious in his ears.

"Years ago, when I was a boy," said Dorian Gray, "you met me, devoted yourself to me, flattered me, and taught me to be vain of my good looks. One day you introduced me to a friend of yours, who explained to me the wonder of youth, and you finished a portrait of me that revealed to me the wonder of beauty. In a mad moment, that I don't know, even now, whether I regret or not, I made a wish. Perhaps you would call it a prayer..."

"I remember it! Oh, how well I remember it! No! the thing is impossible. The room is damp. The mildew has got into the canvas. The paints I used had some wretched mineral poison in them. I tell you the thing is impossible."

"Ah, what is impossible?" murmured the young man, going over to the window, and leaning his forehead against the cold, mist-stained glass.

"You told me you had destroyed it."

"I was wrong. It has destroyed me."

"I don't believe it is my picture."

"Can't you see your romance in it?" said Dorian, bitterly.

"My romance, as you call it..."

"As you called it."

"There was nothing evil in it, nothing shameful. This is the face of a satyr."

"It is the face of my soul."

"God! what a thing I must have worshipped! This has the eyes of a devil."

"Each of us has Heaven and Hell in him, Basil," cried Dorian, with a wild gesture of despair.

Hallward turned again to the portrait, and gazed at it. "My God! if it is true," he exclaimed, "and this is what you have done with your life, why, you must be worse even than those who talk against you fancy you to be!" He held the light up again to the canvas, and examined it. The surface seemed to be quite undisturbed, and as he had left it. It was from within, apparently, that the foulness and horror had come. Through some strange quickening of inner life the leprosies of sin were slowly eating the thing away. The rotting of a corpse in a watery grave was not so fearful.

His hand shook, and the candle fell from its socket on the floor, and lay there sputtering. He placed his foot on it and put it out. Then he flung himself into the rickety chair that was standing by the table and buried his face in his hands.

"Good God, Dorian, what a lesson! what an awful lesson!" There was no answer, but he could hear the young man sobbing at the window.

"Pray, Dorian, pray," he murmured. "What is it that one was taught to say in one's boyhood? 'Lead us not into temptation. Forgive us our sins. Wash away our iniquities.' Let us say that together. The prayer of your pride has been answered. The prayer of your repentance will be answered also. I worshipped you too much. I am punished for it. You worshipped yourself too much. We are both punished."

Dorian Gray turned slowly around, and looked at him with tear-dimmed eyes. "It is too late, Basil," he murmured.

"It is never too late, Dorian. Let us kneel down and try if we can remember a prayer. Isn't there a verse somewhere, 'Though your sins be as scarlet, yet I will make them white as snow'?"

"Those words mean nothing to me now."

"Hush! don't say that. You have done enough evil in your life. My God! don't you see that accursed thing leering at us?"

Dorian Gray glanced at the picture, and suddenly an

uncontrollable feeling of hatred for Basil Hallward came over him. The mad passions of a hunted animal stirred within him, and he loathed the man who was seated at the table, more than he had ever loathed anything in his whole life. He glanced wildly around. Something glimmered on the top of the painted chest that faced him. His eyes fell on it. He knew what it was. It was a knife that he had brought up, some days before, to cut a piece of cord, and had forgotten to take away with him. He moved slowly towards it, passing Hallward as he did so. As soon as he got behind him, he seized it, and turned round. Hallward moved in his chair as if he was going to rise. He rushed at him, and dug the knife into the great vein that is behind the ear, crushing the man's head down on the table, and stabbing again and again.

There was a stifled groan, and the horrible sound of some one choking with blood. The outstretched arms shot up convulsively three times, waving grotesque stiff-fingered hands in the air. He stabbed him once more, but the man did not move. Something began to trickle on the floor. He waited for a moment, still pressing the head down. Then he threw the knife on the table, and listened.

He could hear nothing, but the drip, drip on the threadbare carpet. He opened the door, and went out on the landing. The house was quite quiet. No one was stirring.

He took out the key, and returned to the room, locking himself in as he did so.

The thing was still seated in the chair, straining over the table with bowed head, and humped back, and long fantastic arms. Had it not been for the red jagged tear in the neck, and the clotted black pool that slowly widened on the table, one would have said that the man was simply asleep.

How quickly it had all been done! He felt strangely calm, and, walking over to the window, opened it, and stepped out on the balcony. The wind had blown the fog away, and the sky was like a monstrous peacock's tail, starred with myriads of golden eyes. He looked down, and saw the policeman going his rounds and flashing a bull's-eye lantern on the doors of the silent houses. The crimson spot of a prowling hansom gleamed at the corner, and then vanished. A woman in a ragged shawl was creeping round by the railings, staggering as she went. Now and then she stopped, and peered back. Once, she began to sing in a hoarse voice. The policeman strolled over and said something to her. She stumbled away, laughing. A bitter blast swept across the Square. The gas-lamps flickered, and became blue, and the leafless trees shook their black iron branches as if in pain. He shivered, and went back, closing the window behind him.

He passed to the door, turned the key, and opened it. He did not even glance at the murdered man. He felt that the secret of the whole thing was not to realise the situation. The friend who had painted the fatal portrait, the portrait to which all his misery had been due, had gone out of his life. That was enough.

Then he remembered the lamp. It was a rather curious one of Moorish workmanship, made of dull silver inlaid with arabesques of burnished steel. Perhaps it might be missed by his servant, and questions would be asked. He turned back, and took it from the table. How still the man was! How horribly white the long hands looked! He was like a dreadful wax image.

He locked the door behind him, and crept quietly down-stairs. The wood-work creaked, and seemed to cry out as if in pain. He stopped several times, and waited. No: everything was still. It was merely the sound of his own footsteps.

When he reached the library, he saw the bag and coat in the corner. They must be hidden away somewhere. He unlocked a secret press that was in the wainscoting, and put them into it. He could easily burn them afterwards. Then he pulled out his watch. It was twenty minutes to two.

He sat down, and began to think. Every year – every month,

almost – men were strangled in England for what he had done. There had been a madness of murder in the air. Some red star had come too close to the earth.

Evidence? What evidence was there against him? Basil Hallward had left the house at eleven. No one had seen him come in again. Most of his servants were at Selby Royal. His valet had gone to bed.

Paris! Yes. It was to Paris that Basil had gone by the midnight train, as he had intended. With his curious reserved habits, it would be months before any suspicions would be aroused. Months! Everything could be destroyed long before then.

A sudden thought struck him. He put on his fur coat and hat, and went out into the hall. There he paused, hearing the slow heavy tread of the policeman outside on the pavement, and seeing the flash of the lantern reflected in the window. He waited, holding his breath.

After a few moments he opened the front door, and slipped out, shutting it very gently behind him. Then he began ringing the bell. In about ten minutes his valet appeared, half dressed, and looking very drowsy.

"I am sorry to have had to wake you up, Francis," he said, stepping in, "but I had forgotten my latch-key. What time is it?"

"Five minutes past two, sir," answered the man, looking at the clock and yawning.

"Five minutes past two? How horribly late! You must wake me at nine to-morrow. I have some work to do."

"All right, sir."

"Did any one call this evening?"

"Mr Hallward, sir. He stayed here till eleven, and then he went away to catch his train."

"Oh! I am sorry I didn't see him. Did he leave any message?"

"No, sir, except that he would write to you."

"That will do, Francis. Don't forget to call me at nine to-morrow."

"No, sir."

The man shambled down the passage in his slippers.

Dorian Gray threw his hat and coat upon the yellow marble table, and passed into the library. He walked up and down the room for a quarter of an hour, biting his lip, and thinking. Then he took the Blue Book down from one of the shelves, and began to turn over the leaves. "Alan Campbell, 152, Hertford Street, Mayfair". Yes; that was the man he wanted.

TWELVE

At nine o'clock the next morning his servant came in with a cup of chocolate on a tray, and opened the shutters. Dorian was sleeping quite peacefully, lying on his right side, with one hand underneath his cheek. He looked like a boy who had been tired out with play, or study.

The man had to touch him twice on the shoulder before he woke, and as he opened his eyes a faint smile passed across his lips, as though he had been having some delightful dream. Yet he had not dreamed at all. His night had been untroubled by any images of pleasure or pain. But youth smiles without any reason. It is one of its chiefest charms.

He turned round, and, leaning on his elbow, began to drink his chocolate. The mellow November sun was streaming into the room. The sky was bright blue, and there was a genial warmth in the air. It was almost like a morning in May.

Gradually the events of the preceding night crept with silent bloodstained feet into his brain, and reconstructed themselves there with terrible distinctness. He winced at the memory of all that he had suffered, and for a moment the same curious feeling of loathing for Basil Hallward, that had made him kill him as he sat in the chair, came back to him, and he grew cold with passion. The dead man was still sitting there, too, and in the sunlight now. How horrible that was! Such hideous things were for the darkness, not for the day.

He felt that if he brooded on what he had gone through he would sicken or grow mad. There were sins whose fascination was more in the memory that in the doing of them, strange triumphs that gratified the pride more than the passions, and gave to the intellect a quickened sense of joy, greater than any joy they brought, or could ever bring, to the senses. But this was not one of them. It was a thing to be driven out of the mind, to be drugged with poppies, to be strangled lest it might strangle one itself.

He passed his hand across his forehead, and then got up hastily, and dressed himself with even more than his usual attention, giving a good deal of care to the selection of his necktie and scarf-pin, and changing his rings more than once.

He spent a long time over breakfast, tasting the various dishes, talking to his valet about some new liveries that he was thinking of getting made for the servants at Selby, and going through his correspondence. Over some of the letters he smiled. Three of them bored him. One he read several times over, and then tore up with a slight look of annoyance in his face. "That awful thing, a woman's memory!" as Lord Henry had once said.

When he had drunk his coffee, he sat down at the table, and wrote two letters. One he put in his pocket, the other he handed to the valet.

"Take this round to 152, Hertford Street, Francis, and if Mr. Campbell is out of town, get his address."

As soon as he was alone, he lit a cigarette, and began sketching upon a piece of paper, drawing flowers, and bits of architecture, first, and then faces. Suddenly he remarked that every face that he drew seemed to have an extraordinary likeness to Basil Hallward. He frowned, and, getting up, went over to the bookcase and took out a volume at hazard. He was determined that he would not think about what had happened, till it became absolutely necessary to do so.

When he had stretched himself on the sofa, he looked at the title-page of the book. It was Gautier's 'Emaux et Camées', Charpentier's Japanese paper edition, with the Jacquemart etching. The binding was of citron-green leather with a design of gilt trellis-work and dotted pomegranates. It had been given to him by Adrian Singleton. As he turned over the pages his eye fell on the poem about the hand of Lacenaire, the cold yellow hand 'du supplice encore mal lavée', with its downy red hairs and its 'doigts de faune'. He glanced at his own white taper fingers, and passed on, till he came to those lovely verses upon Venice:

> *Sur une gamme chromatique*
> *Le sein de perles ruisselant*
> *La Vénus de l'Adriatique*
> *Sort de l'eau son corps rose et blanc.*
>
> *Les dômes, sur l'azur des ondes*
> *Suivant la phrase au pur contour,*
> *S'enflent comme des gorges rondes*
> *Que soulève un soupir d'amour.*
>
> *L'esquif aborde et me dépose,*
> *Jetant some amarre au pilier,*
> *Devant une façade rose,*
> *Sur le marbre d'un escalier.*

How exquisite they were! As one read them, one seemed to be floating down the green water-ways of the pink and pearl city, lying in a black gondola with silver prow and trailing curtains. The mere lines looked to him like those straight lines of turquoise-blue that follow one as one pushes out to the Lido. The sudden flashes of colour reminded him of the gleam of the opal-and-iris-throated birds that flutter round the tall honey-combed Campanile, or stalk, with such stately grace, through the dim arcades. Leaning back with half-closed eyes, he kept saying over and over to himself –

> *Devant une façade rose,*
> *Sur le marbre d'un escalier.*

The whole of Venice was in those two lines. He remembered the autumn that he had passed there, and a wonderful love that had stirred him to delightful fantastic follies. There was romance in every place. But Venice, like Oxford, had kept the background for romance, and background was everything or almost everything. Basil had been with him part of the time, and had gone wild over Tintoret. Poor Basil! what a horrible way for a man to die!

He sighed, and took up the book again, and tried to forget. He read of the swallows that fly in and out of the little café at Smyrna where the Hadjis sit counting their amber beads and the turbaned merchants smoke their long tasselled pipes and talk gravely to each other; of the Obelisk in the Place de la Concorde that weeps tears of granite in its lonely sunless exile, and longs to be back by the hot lotus-covered Nile, where there are Sphinxes, and rose-red ibises, and white vultures with gilded claws, and crocodiles, with small beryl eyes, that crawl over the green steaming mud; and of that curious statue that Gautier compares to a contralto voice, the 'monstre charmant' that couches in the porphyry-room of the Louvre. But after a time the book fell from his hand. He grew nervous, and a horrible fit of terror came over him. What if Alan Campbell should be out of England? Days would elapse before he could come back. Perhaps he might refuse to come. What could he do then? Every moment was of vital importance.

They had been great friends once, five years before – almost inseparable, indeed. Then the intimacy had come suddenly to an end. When they met in society now, it was only Dorian Gray who smiled: Alan Campbell never did.

He was an extremely clever young man, though he had no real appreciation of the visible arts, and whatever little sense of the beauty of poetry he possessed he had gained entirely from Dorian. His dominant intellectual passion was for science. At Cambridge he had spent a great deal of his time working in the Laboratory, and had taken a good class in the Natural Science tripos of his year. Indeed, he was still devoted to the study of chemistry, and had a laboratory of his own, in which he used to shut himself up all day long, greatly to the annoyance of his mother, who had set her heart on his standing for Parliament and had a vague idea that a chemist was a person who made up prescriptions. He was an excellent musician, however, as well, and played both the violin and the piano better than most amateurs. In fact, it was music that had first brought him and Dorian Gray together – music and that indefinable attraction that Dorian seemed to be able to exercise whenever he wished, and indeed exercised often without being conscious of it. They had met at Lady Berkshire's the night that Rubinstein played there, and after that used to be always seen together at the Opera, and wherever good music was going on. For eighteen months their intimacy lasted. Campbell was always either at Selby Royal or in Grosvenor Square. To him, as to many others, Dorian Gray was the type of everything that is wonderful and fascinating in life. Whether or not a quarrel had taken place between them no one ever knew. But suddenly people remarked that they scarcely spoke when they met, and that Campbell seemed always to go away early from any party at which Dorian Gray was present. He had changed, too – was strangely melancholy at times, appeared almost to dislike hearing music of any passionate character, and would never himself play, giving as his excuse, when he was called upon, that he was so absorbed in science that he had no time left in which to practice. And this was certainly true. Every day he seemed to become more interested in biology, and his name appeared once or twice in some of the scientific reviews, in connection with certain curious experiments.

This was the man that Dorian Gray was waiting for, pacing up and down the room, glancing every moment at the clock, and becoming horribly agitated as the minutes went by. At last the door opened, and his servant entered.

"Mr. Alan Campbell, sir."

A sigh of relief broke from his parched lips, and the colour came back to his cheeks.

"Ask him to come in at once, Francis."

The man bowed, and retired. In a few moments, Alan Campbell walked in, looking very stern and rather pale, his pallor being intensified by his coal-black hair and dark eyebrows.

"Alan! this is kind of you. I thank you for coming."

"I had intended never to enter your house again, Gray. But you said it was a matter of life and death." His voice was hard and cold. He spoke with slow deliberation. There was a look of contempt in the steady searching gaze that he turned on Dorian. He kept his hands in the pockets of his Astrakhan coat, and appeared not to have noticed the gesture with which he had been greeted.

"It is a matter of life and death, Alan, and to more than one person. Sit down."

Campbell took a chair by the table, and Dorian sat opposite to him. The two men's eyes met. In Dorian's there was infinite pity. He knew that what he was going to do was dreadful.

After a strained moment of silence, he leaned across and said, very quietly, but watching the effect of each word upon the face of the man he had sent for, "Alan, in a locked room at the top of this house, a room to which nobody but myself has access, a dead man is seated at a table. He has been dead ten hours now. Don't stir, and don't look at me like that. Who the man is, why he died, how he died, are matters that do not concern you. What you have to do is this—"

"Stop, Gray. I don't want to know anything further. Whether what you have told me is true or not true, doesn't concern me. I entirely decline to be mixed up in your life. Keep your horrible secrets to yourself. They don't interest me any more."

"Alan, they will have to interest you. This one will have to interest you. I am awfully sorry for you, Alan. But I can't help myself. You are the one man who is able to save me. I am forced to bring you into the matter. I have no option. Alan, you are a scientist. You know about chemistry, and things of that kind. You have made experiments. What you have got to do is to destroy the thing that is up-stairs – to destroy it so that not a vestige will be left of it. Nobody saw this person come into the house. Indeed, at the present moment he is supposed to be in Paris. He will not be missed for months. When he is missed, there must be no trace of him found here. You, Alan, you must change him, and everything that belongs to him, into a handful of ashes that I may scatter in the air."

"You are mad, Dorian."

"Ah! I was waiting for you to call me Dorian."

"You are mad, I tell you – mad to imagine that I would raise a finger to help you, mad to make this monstrous confession. I will have nothing to do with this matter, whatever it is. Do you think I am going to peril my reputation for you? What is it to me what devil's work you are up to?"

"It was a suicide, Alan."

"I am glad of that. But who drove him to it? You, I should fancy."

"Do you still refuse to do this, for me?"

"Of course I refuse. I will have absolutely nothing to do with it. I don't care what shame comes on you. You deserve it all. I should not be sorry to see you disgraced, publicly disgraced. How dare you ask me, of all men in the world, to mix myself up in this horror? I should have thought you knew more about people's characters. Your friend Lord Henry Wotton can't have taught you much about psychology, whatever else he has taught you. Nothing will induce me to stir a step to help you. You have come to the wrong man. Go to some of your friends. Don't come to me."

"Alan, it was murder. I killed him. You don't know what he had made me suffer. Whatever my life is, he had more to do with the making or the marring of it than poor Harry has had. He may not have intended it, the result was the same."

"Murder! Good God, Dorian, is that what you have come to? I shall not inform upon you. It is not my business. Besides, you are certain to be arrested, without my stirring in the matter. Nobody ever commits a murder without doing something stupid. But I will have nothing to do with it."

"All I ask of you is to perform a certain scientific experiment. You go to hospitals and dead-houses, and the horrors that you do there don't affect you. If in some hideous dissecting-room or fetid laboratory you found this man lying on a leaden table with red gutters scooped out in it, you would simply look upon him as an admirable subject. You would not turn a hair. You would not believe that you were doing anything wrong. On the contrary, you would probably feel that you were benefiting the human race, or increasing the sum or knowledge in the world, or gratifying intellectual curiosity, or something of that kind. What I want you to do is simply what you have often done before. Indeed, to destroy a body must be less horrible than what you are accustomed to work at. And, remember, it is the only piece of evidence against me. If it is discovered, I am lost; and it is sure to be discovered unless you help me."

"I have no desire to help you. You forget that. I am simply indifferent to the whole thing. It has nothing to do with me."

"Alan, I entreat you. Think of the position I am in. Just before you came I almost fainted with terror. No! don't think of that. Look at the matter purely from the scientific point of view. You don't inquire where the dead things on which you experiment come from. Don't inquire now. I have told you too much as it is. But I beg of you to do this. We were friends once, Alan."

"Don't speak about those days, Dorian: they are dead."

"The dead linger sometimes. The man up-stairs will not go away. He is sitting at the table with bowed head and outstretched arms. Alan! Alan! if you don't come to my assistance I am ruined. Why, they will hang me, Alan! Don't you understand? They will hang me for what I have done."

"There is no good in prolonging this scene. I refuse absolutely to do anything in the matter. It is insane of you to ask me."

"You refuse absolutely?"

"Yes."

The same look of pity came into Dorian's eyes, then he stretched out his hand, took a piece of paper, and wrote something on it. He read it over twice, folded it carefully, and pushed it across the table. Having done this, he got up, and went over to the window.

Campbell looked at him in surprise, and then took up the paper, and opened it. As he read it, his face became ghastly pale, and he fell back in his chair. A horrible sense of sickness came over him. He felt as if his heart was beating itself to death in some empty hollow.

After two or three minutes of terrible silence, Dorian turned round and came and stood behind him, putting his hand upon his shoulder.

"I am so sorry, Alan," he murmured, "but you leave me no alternative. I have a letter written already. Here it is. You see the address. If you don't help me, I must send it. You know what the result will be. But you are going to help me. It is impossible for you to refuse now. I tried to spare you. You will do me the justice to admit that. You were stern, harsh, offensive. You treated me as no man has ever dared to treat me – no living man, at any rate. I bore it all. Now it is for me to dictate terms."

Campbell buried his face in this hands, and a shudder passed through him.

"Yes, it is my turn to dictate terms, Alan. You know what they are. The thing is quite simple. Come, don't work yourself into this fever. The thing has to be done. Face it, and do it."

A groan broke from Campbell's lips, and he shivered all over. The ticking of the clock on the mantelpiece seemed to him to be dividing time into separate atoms of agony, each of which was too terrible to be borne. He felt as if an iron ring was being slowly tightened round his forehead, and as if the disgrace with which he was threatened had already come upon him. The hand upon his shoulder weighed like a hand of lead. It was intolerable. It seemed to crush him.

"Come, Alan, you must decide at once."

He hesitated a moment. "Is there a fire in the room up-stairs?" he murmured.

"Yes, there is a gas-fire with asbestos."

"I will have to go home and get some things from the laboratory."

"No, Alan, you will not leave the house. Write on a sheet of notepaper what you want, and my servant will take a cab and bring the things back to you."

Campbell wrote a few lines, blotted them, and addressed the envelope to his assistant. Dorian took the note up and read it carefully. Then he rang the bell, and gave it to his valet, with orders to return as soon as possible, and to bring the things with him.

When the hall door shut, Campbell started, and, having got up from the chair, went over to the chimney-piece. He was shivering with a sort of ague. For nearly twenty minutes, neither of the men spoke. A fly buzzed noisily about the room, and the ticking of the clock was like the beat of a hammer.

As the chime struck one, Campbell turned around, and,

looking at Dorian Gray, saw that his eyes were filled with tears. There was something in the purity and the refinement of that sad face that seemed to enrage him. "You are infamous, absolutely infamous!" he muttered.

"Hush, Alan: you have saved my life," said Dorian.

"'Your' life? Good heavens! what a life that is! You have gone from corruption to corruption, and now you have culminated in crime. In doing what I am going to do, what you force me to do, it is not 'your' life that I am thinking."

"Ah, Alan," murmured Dorian, with a sigh, "I wish you had a thousandth part of the pity for me that I have for you." He turned away, as he spoke, and stood looking out at the garden. Campbell made no answer.

After about ten minutes a knock came to the door, and the servant entered, carrying a mahogany chest of chemicals, with a small electric battery set on top of it. He placed it on the table, and went out again, returning with a long coil of steel and platinum wire and two rather curiously-shaped iron clamps.

"Shall I leave the things here, sir?" he asked Campbell.

"Yes," said Dorian. "And I am afraid, Francis, that I have another errand for you. What is the name of the man at Richmond who supplies Selby with orchids?"

"Harden, sir?"

"Yes – Harden. You must go down to Richmond at once, see Harden personally, and tell him to send twice as many orchids as I ordered, and to have as few white ones as possible. In fact, I don't want any white ones. It is a lovely day, Francis, and Richmond is a very pretty place, otherwise I wouldn't bother you about it."

"No trouble, sir. At what time shall I be back?"

Dorian looked at Campbell. "How long will your experiment take, Alan?" he said, in a calm, indifferent voice. The presence of a third person in the room seemed to give him extraordinary courage.

Campbell frowned, and bit his lip. "It will take about five hours," he answered.

"It will be time enough, then, if you are back at half-past seven, Francis. Or stay: just leave my things out for dressing. You can have the evening to yourself. I am not dining at home, so I shall not want you."

"Thank you, sir," said the man, leaving the room.

"Now, Alan, there is not a moment to be lost. How heavy this chest is! I'll take it for you. You bring the other things." He spoke rapidly, and in an authoritative manner. Campbell felt dominated by him. They left the room together.

When they reached the top landing, Dorian took out the key and turned it in the lock. Then he stopped, and a troubled look came into his eyes. He shuddered. "I don't think I can go in, Alan," he murmured.

"It is nothing to me. I don't require you," said Campbell, coldly.

Dorian half opened the door. As he did so, he saw the face of the portrait grinning in the sunlight. On the floor in front of it the torn curtain was lying. He remembered that the night before, for the first time in his life, he had forgotten to hide it, when he crept out of the room.

But what was that loathsome red dew that gleamed, wet and glistening, on one of the hands, as though the canvas had sweated blood? How horrible it was! – more horrible, it seemed to him for the moment, than the silent thing that he knew was stretched across the table, the thing whose grotesque misshapen shadow on the spotted carpet showed him that it had not stirred, but was still there, as he had left it.

He opened the door a little wider, and walked quickly in, with half-closed eyes and averted head, determined that he would not look even once upon the dead man. Then, stooping down, and taking up the gold-and-purple hanging, he flung it over the picture.

He stopped, feeling afraid to turn round, and his eyes fixed themselves on the intricacies of the pattern before him. He heard Campbell bringing in the heavy chest, and the irons, and the other things that he had required for his dreadful work. He began to wonder if he and Basil Hallward had ever met, and, if so, what they had thought of each other.

"Leave me now," said Campbell.

He turned and hurried out, just conscious that the dead man had been thrust back into the chair and was sitting up in it, with Campbell gazing into the glistening yellow face. As he was going downstairs he heard the key being turned in the lock.

It was long after seven o'clock when Campbell came back into the library. He was pale, but absolutely calm. "I have done what you asked me to do," he muttered. "And now, good-bye. Let us never see each other again."

"You have saved me from ruin, Alan. I cannot forget that," said Dorian, simply.

As soon as Campbell had left, he went upstairs. There was a horrible smell of chemicals in the room. But the thing that had been sitting at the table was gone.

THIRTEEN

"There is no good telling me you are going to be good, Dorian," cried Lord Henry, dipping his white fingers into a red copper bowl filled with rose-water. "You are quite perfect. Pray don't change."

Dorian shook his head. "No, Harry, I have done too many dreadful things in my life. I am not going to do any more. I began my good actions yesterday."

"Where were you yesterday?"

"In the country, Harry. I was staying at a little inn by myself."

"My dear boy," said Lord Henry smiling, "any-body can be good in the country. There are no temptations there. That is the reason why people who live out of town are so uncivilised. There are only two ways, as you know, of becoming civilised. One is by being cultured, the other is by being corrupt. Country-people have no opportunity of being either, so they stagnate."

"Culture and corruption," murmured Dorian. "I have known something of both. It seems to me curious now that they should ever be found together. For I have a new ideal, Harry. I am going to alter. I think I have altered."

"You have not told me yet what your good action was. Or did you say you had done more than one?"

"I can tell you, Harry. It is not a story I could tell to any one else. I spared somebody. She was quite beautiful, and wonderfully like Sibyl Vane. I think it was that which first attracted me to her. You remember Sibyl, don't you? How long ago that seems! Well, Hetty was not one of our class, of course. She was simply a girl in a village. But I really loved her. I am quite sure that I loved her. All during this wonderful May that we have been having, I used to run down and see her two or three times a week. Yesterday she met me in a little orchard. The apple-blossoms kept tumbling down on her hair, and she was laughing. We were to have gone away together this morning at dawn. Suddenly I determined to leave her as flower-like as I had found her."

"I should think the novelty of the emotion must have given you a thrill of real pleasure, Dorian," interrupted Lord Henry. "But I can finish your idyll for you. You gave her good advice, and broke her heart. That was the beginning of your reformation."

"Harry, you are horrible! You mustn't say these dreadful things. Hetty's heart is not broken. Of course she cried, and all that. But there is no disgrace upon her. She can live, like Perdita, in her garden."

"And weep over a faithless Florizel," said Lord Henry, laughing. "My dear Dorian, you have the most curiously boyish moods. Do you think this girl will ever be really contented now with any one of her own rank? I suppose she will be married some day to a rough carter or a grinning ploughman. Well, having met you, and loved you, will teach her to despise her husband, and she will be wretched. From a moral point of view I really don't think much of your great renunciation. Even as a beginning, it is poor. Besides, how do you know that Hetty isn't floating at the present moment in some millpond, with water-lilies round her like Ophelia?"

"I can't bear this, Harry! You mock at everything, and then suggest the most serious tragedies. I am sorry I told you now. I don't care what you say to me, I know I was right in acting as I did. Poor

Hetty! As I rode past the farm this morning, I saw her white face at the window, like a spray of jasmine. Don't let me talk about it any more, and don't try to persuade me that the first good action I have done for years, the first little bit of self-sacrifice I have ever known, is really a sort of sin. I want to be better. I am going to be better. Tell me something about yourself. What is going on in town? I have not been to the club for days."

"The people are still discussing poor Basil's disappearance."

"I should have thought they had got tired of that by this time," said Dorian, pouring himself out some wine, and frowning slightly.

"My dear boy, they have only been talking about it for six weeks, and the public are really not equal to the mental strain of having more than one topic every three months. They have been very fortunate lately, however. They have had my own divorce-case, and Alan Campbell's suicide. Now they have got the mysterious disappearance of an artist. Scotland Yard still insists that the man in the grey ulster who left Victoria by the midnight train on the 7th November was poor Basil, and the French police declare that Basil never arrived in Paris at all. I suppose in about a fortnight we will be told that he has been seen in San Francisco. It is an odd thing, but every one who disappears is said to be seen at San Francisco. It must be a delightful city, and possess all the attractions of the next world."

"What do you think has happened to Basil?" asked Dorian, holding up his Burgundy against the light, and wondering how it was that he could discuss the matter so calmly.

"I have not the slightest idea. If Basil chooses to hide himself, it is no business of mine. If he is dead, I don't want to think about him. Death is the only thing that ever terrifies me. I hate it. One can survive everything nowadays except that. Death and vulgarity are the only two facts in the nineteenth century that one cannot explain away. Let us have our coffee in the music-room,

Dorian. You must play Chopin to me. The man with whom my wife ran away played Chopin exquisitely. Poor Victoria! I was very fond of her. The house is rather lonely without her."

Dorian said nothing, but rose from the table, and, passing into the next room, sat down to the piano and let his fingers stray across the keys. After the coffee had been brought in, he stopped, and, looking over at Lord Henry, said, "Harry, did it ever occur to you that Basil was murdered?"

Lord Henry yawned. "Basil had no enemies, and always wore a Waterbury watch. Why should he be murdered? He was not clever enough to have enemies. Of course he had a wonderful genius for painting. But a man can paint like Velasquez and yet be as dull as possible. Basil was really rather dull. He only interested me once, and that was when he told me, years ago, that he had a wild adoration for you."

"I was very fond of Basil," said Dorian, with a sad look in his eyes. "But don't people say that he was murdered?"

"Oh, some of the papers do. It does not seem to be probable. I know there are dreadful places in Paris, but Basil was not the sort of man to have gone to them. He had no curiosity. It was his chief defect. Play me a nocturne, Dorian, and, as you play, tell me, in a low voice, how you have kept your youth. You must have some secret. I am only ten years older than you are, and I am wrinkled, and bald, and yellow. You are really wonderful, Dorian. You have never looked more charming than you do to-night. You remind me of the day I saw you first. You were rather cheeky, very shy, and absolutely extraordinary. You have changed, of course, but not in appearance. I wish you would tell me your secret. To get back my youth I would do anything in the world, except take exercise, get up early, or be respectable. Youth! There is nothing like it. It's absurd to talk of the ignorance of youth. The only people whose opinions I listen to now with any respect are people must younger than myself. They seem in front of me. Life has revealed to them her last wonder. As for the aged, I always contradict the aged. I do it on principle. If you ask them their opinion on something that happened yesterday, they solemnly give you the opinions current in 1820, when people wore high stocks and knew absolutely nothing. How lovely that thing you are playing is! I wonder did Chopin write it at Majorca, with the sea weeping round the villa, and the salt spray dashing against the panes? It is marvellously romantic. What a blessing it is that there is one art left to us that is not imitative! Don't stop. I want music to-night. It seems to me that you are the young Apollo, and that I am Marsyas listening to you. I have sorrows, Dorian, of my own, that even you know nothing of. The tragedy of old age is not that one is old, but that one is young. I am amazed sometimes at my own sincerity. Ah, Dorian, how happy you are! What an exquisite life you have had! You have drunk deeply of everything. You have crushed the grapes against your palate. Nothing has been hidden from you. But it has all been to you no more than the sound of music. It has not marred you. You are still the same.

"I wonder what the rest of your life will be. Don't spoil it by renunciations. At present you are a perfect type. Don't make yourself incomplete. You are quite flawless now. You need not shake your head: you know you are. Besides, Dorian, don't deceive yourself. Life is not governed by will or intention. Life is a question of nerves, and fibres, and slowly-built-up cells in which thought hides itself and passion has its dreams. You may fancy yourself safe, and think yourself strong. But a chance tone of colour in a room or a morning sky, a particular perfume that you had once loved and that brings strange memories with it, a line from a forgotten poem that you had come across again, a cadence from a piece of music that you had ceased to play – I tell you, Dorian, that it is on things like these that our lives depend. Browning writes about that somewhere; but our own senses will imagine them for us. There are moments when the odour of heliotrope passes suddenly across me, and I have to live the strangest year of my life over again.

"I wish I could change places with you, Dorian. The world has cried out against us both, but it has always worshipped you. It always will worship you. You are the type of what the age is searching for, and what it is afraid it has found. I am so glad that you have never done anything, never carved a statue, or painted a picture, or produced anything outside of yourself! Life has been your art. You have set yourself to music. Your days have been your sonnets."

Dorian rose up from the piano, and passed his hand through his hair. "Yes, life has been exquisite," he murmured, "but I am not going to have the same life, Harry. And you must not say these extravagant things to me. You don't know everything about me. I think that if you did, even you would turn from me. You laugh. Don't laugh."

"Why have you stopped playing, Dorian? Go back and play the nocturne over again. Look at that great honey-coloured moon that hangs in the dusky air. She is waiting for you to charm her, and if you play she will come closer to the earth. You won't? Let us go to the club, then. It has been a charming evening, and we must end it charmingly. There is some one at the club who wants immensely to know you – young Lord Poole, Bournmouth's eldest son. He has already copied your neckties, and has begged me to introduce him to you. He is quite delightful, and rather reminds me of you."

"I hope not," said Dorian, with a touch of pathos in his voice. "But I am tired to-night, Harry. I won't go to the club. It is nearly eleven, and I want to go to bed early."

"Do stay. You have never played so well as to-night. There was something in your touch that was wonderful. It had more expression than I had ever heard from it before."

"It is because I am going to be good," he answered smiling. "I am a little changed already."

"Don't change, Dorian; at any rate, don't change to me. We

must always be friends."

"Yet you poisoned me with a book once. I should not forgive that. Harry, promise me that you will never lend that book to any one. It does harm."

"My dear boy, you are really beginning to moralise. You will soon be going about warning people against all the sins of which you have grown tired. You are much too delightful to do that. Besides, it is no use. You and I are what we are, and will be what we will be. Come round to-morrow. I am going to ride at eleven, and we might go together. The Park is quite lovely now. I don't think there have been such lilacs since the year I met you."

"Very well. I will be here at eleven," said Dorian. "Good-night, Harry." As he reached the door he hesitated for a moment, as if he had something more to say. Then he sighed and went out.

It was a lovely night, so warm that he threw his coat over his arm, and did not even put his silk scarf round his throat. As he strolled home, smoking his cigarette, two young men in evening dress passed him. He heard one of them whisper to the other, "That is Dorian Gray." He remembered how pleased he used to be when he was pointed out, or stared at, or talked about. He was tired of hearing his own name now. Half the charm of the little village where he had been so often lately was that no one knew who he was. He had told the girl whom he had made love him that he was poor, and she had believed him. He had told her once that he was wicked, and she had laughed at him, and told him that wicked people were always very old and very ugly. What a laugh she had! – just like a thrush singing. And how pretty she had been in her cotton dresses and her large hats! She knew nothing, but she had everything that he had lost.

When he reached home, he found his servant waiting up for him. He sent him to bed, and threw himself down on the sofa in the library, and began to think over some of the things that Lord

Henry had said to him.

Was it really true that one could never change? He felt a wild longing for the unsustained purity of his boyhood – his rose-white boyhood, as Lord Henry had once called it. He knew that he had tarnished himself, filled his mind with corruption, and given horror to his fancy; that he had been an evil influence to others, and had experienced a terrible joy in being so; and that of the lives that had crossed his own it had been the fairest and the most full of promise that he had brought to shame. But was it all irretrievable? Was there no hope for him?

It was better not to think of the past. Nothing could alter that. It was of himself, and of his own future, that he had to think. Alan Campbell had shot himself one night in his laboratory, but had not revealed the secret that he had been forced to know. The excitement, such as it was, over Basil Hallward's disappearance would soon pass away. It was already waning. He was perfectly safe there. Nor, indeed, was it the death of Basil Hallward that weighed most upon his mind. It was the living death of his own soul that troubled him. Basil had painted the portrait that had marred his life. He could not forgive that. It was the portrait that had done everything. Basil had said things to him that were unbearable, and that he had yet borne with patience. The murder had been simply the madness of a moment. As for Alan Campbell, his suicide had been his own act. He had chosen to do it. It was nothing to him.

A new life! That was what he wanted. That was what he was waiting for. Surely he had begun it already. He had spared one innocent thing, at any rate. He would never again tempt innocence. He would be good.

As he thought of Hetty Merton, he began to wonder if the portrait in the locked room had changed. Surely it was not still so horrible as it had been? Perhaps if his life became pure, he would be able to expel every sign of evil passion from the face. Perhaps the signs of evil had gone away. He would go and look.

He took the lamp from the table and crept upstairs. As he unlocked the door, a smile of joy flitted across his young face and lingered for a moment about his lips. Yes, he would be good, and the hideous thing that he had hidden away would no longer be a terror to him. He felt as if the load had been lifted from him already.

He went in quietly, locking the door behind him, as was his custom, and dragged the purple hanging from the portrait. A cry of pain and indignation broke from him. He could see no change, unless that in the eyes there was a look of cunning, and in the mouth the curved wrinkle of the hypocrite. The thing was still loathsome - more loathsome, if possible, than before - and the scarlet dew that spotted the hand seemed brighter, and more like blood newly spilt.

Had it been merely vanity that had made him do his one good deed? Or the desire of a new sensation, as Lord Henry had hinted, with his mocking laugh? Or that passion to act a part that sometimes makes us do things finer than we are ourselves? Or, perhaps, all these?

Why was the red stain larger than it had been? It seemed to have crept like a horrible disease over the wrinkled fingers. There was blood on the painted feet, as though the thing had dripped - blood even on the hand that had not held the knife.

Confess? Did it mean that he was to confess? To give himself up, and be put to death? He laughed. He felt that the idea was monstrous. Besides, who would believe him, even if he did confess? There was no trace of the murdered man anywhere. Everything belonging to him had been destroyed. He himself had burned what had been below-stairs. The world would simply say he was mad. They would shut him up if he persisted in his story.

Yet it was his duty to confess, to suffer public shame, and to make public atonement. There was a God who called upon men to tell their sins to earth as well as to heaven. Nothing that he could do would cleanse him till he had told his own sin. His sin? He shrugged his shoulders. The death of Basil Hallward seemed very little to him. He was thinking of Hetty Merton.

It was an unjust mirror, this mirror of his soul that he was looking at. Vanity? Curiosity? Hypocrisy? Had there been nothing more in his renunciation than that? There had been something more. At least he thought so. But who could tell?

And this murder – was it to dog him all his life? Was he never to get rid of the past? Was he really to confess? No. There was only one bit of evidence left against him. The picture itself – that was evidence.

He would destroy it. Why had he kept it so long? It had given him pleasure once to watch it changing and growing old. Of late he had felt no such pleasure. It had kept him awake at night. When he had been away, he had been filled with terror lest other eyes should look upon it. It had brought melancholy across his passions. Its mere memory had marred many moments of joy. It had been like conscience to him. Yes, it had been conscience. He would destroy it.

He looked round, and saw the knife that had stabbed Basil Hallward. He had cleaned it many times, till there was no stain left upon it. It was bright, and glistened. As it had killed the painter, so it would kill the painter's work, and all that that meant. It would kill the past, and when that was dead he would be free. He seized it, and stabbed the canvas with it, ripping the thing right up from top to bottom.

There was a cry heard, and a crash. The cry was so horrible in its agony that the frightened servants woke, and crept out of their rooms. Two gentlemen, who were passing in the Square below, stopped and looked up at the great house. They walked on till they met a policeman, and brought him back. The man rang the bell several times, but there was no answer. The house was all dark, except for a light in one of the top windows. After a time, he went away, and stood in the portico of the next house and watched.

"Whose house is that, constable?" asked the elder of the two gentlemen.

"Mr. Dorian Gray's, sir," answered the policeman.

They looked at each other, as they walked away, and sneered. One of them was Sir Henry Ashton's uncle.

Inside, in the servants' part of the house, the half-clad domestics were talking in low whispers to each other. Old Mrs. Leaf was crying, and wringing her hands. Francis was as pale as death.

After about a quarter of an hour, he got the coachman and one of the footmen and crept up-stairs. They knocked, but there was no reply. They called out. Everything was still. Finally, after vainly trying to force the door, they got on the roof, and dropped down on to the balcony. The windows yielded easily: the bolts were old.

When they entered, they found hanging upon the wall a splendid portrait of their master as they had last seen him, in all the wonder of his exquisite youth and beauty. Lying on the floor was a dead man in evening dress, with a knife in his heart. He was withered, wrinkled and loathsome of visage. It was not till they examined the rings that they recognised who he was.

APPENDIX ONE:
THE PREFACE TO THE
1891 EDITION

The artist is the creator of beautiful things.
To reveal art and conceal the artist is art's aim.

The critic is he who can translate into another manner or a
new material his impression of beautiful things.

The highest as the lowest form of criticism is a mode
of autobiography.

Those who find ugly meanings in beautiful things are
corrupt without being charming. This is a fault.

Those who find beautiful meanings in beautiful
things are cultivated. For these there is hope.

They are the elect to whom beautiful things mean only beauty.

There is no such thing as a moral or an immoral
book. Books are well written, or badly written. That is all.

The nineteenth century dislike of realism is the rage of Caliban seeing his own face in a glass.

The nineteenth century dislike of romanticism is
the rage of Caliban not seeing his own face in a glass.

The moral life of man forms part of the subject-matter
of the artist, but the morality of art consists in the perfect use of an imperfect medium.

No artist desires to prove anything. Even things that are true can be proved.

No artist has ethical sympathies. An ethical sympathy
in an artist is an unpardonable mannerism of style.

No artist is ever morbid. The artist can express everything.

Thought and language are to the artist instruments of
an art.

Vice and virtue are to the artist materials for an art.

From the point of view of form, the type of all the arts is
the art of the musician. From the point of view of feeling, the actor's craft is the type.

All art is at once surface and symbol.

Those who go beneath the surface do so at their peril.

Those who read the symbol do so at their peril.

It is the spectator, and not life, that art really mirrors.

Diversity of opinion about a work of art shows that the work is new, complex, and vital.

When critics disagree, the artist is in accord with himself.

We can forgive a man for making a useful thing as long as he does not admire it. The only excuse for making a useless thing is that one admires it intensely.

All art is quite useless.

APPENDIX TWO:
CHAPTER XVI FROM THE 1891 EDITION

Cold rain began to fall, and the blurred street-lamps looked ghastly in the dripping mist. The public-houses were just closing, and dim men and women were clustering in broken groups round their doors. From some of the bars came the sound of horrible laughter. In others, drunkards brawled and screamed.

Lying back in the hansom, with his hat pulled over his forehead, Dorian Gray watched with listless eyes the sordid shame of the great city, and now and then he repeated to himself the words that Lord Henry had said to him on the first day they had met, "To cure the soul by means of the senses, and the senses by means of the soul". Yes, that was the secret. He had often tried it, and would try it again now. There were opium dens, where one could buy oblivion, dens of horror where the memory of old sins could be destroyed by the madness of sins that were new.

The moon hung low in the sky like a yellow skull. From time to time a huge misshapen cloud stretched a long arm across and hid it. The gas-lamps grew fewer, and the streets more narrow and gloomy. Once the man lost his way, and had to drive back half a mile. A steam rose from the horse as it splashed up the puddles. The side-windows of the hansom were clogged with a grey-flannel mist.

"To cure the soul by means of the senses, and the senses by means of the soul!" How the words rang in his ears! His soul, certainly, was sick to death. Was it true that the senses could cure it? Innocent blood had been spilt. What could atone for that? Ah, for that there was no atonement; but though forgiveness was impossible, forgetfulness was possible still, and he was determined to forget, to stamp the thing out, to crush it as one would crush the adder that had stung one. Indeed, what right had Basil to have spoken to him as he had done? Who had made him a judge over others? He had said things that were dreadful, horrible, not to be endured.

On and on plodded the hansom, going slower, it seemed to him, at each step. He thrust up the trap, and called to the man to drive faster. The hideous hunger for opium began to gnaw at him. His throat burned, and his delicate hands twitched nervously together. He struck at the horse madly with his stick. The driver laughed, and whipped up. He laughed in answer, and the man was silent.

The way seemed interminable, and the streets like the black web of some sprawling spider. The monotony became unbearable and, as the mist thickened, he felt afraid.

Then they passed by lonely brickfields. The fog was lighter here, and he could see the strange bottle-shaped kilns with their orange fan-like tongues of fire. A dog barked as they went by, and far away in the darkness some wandering seagull screamed. The horse stumbled in a rut, then swerved aside, and broke into a gallop.

After some time they left the clay road, and rattled again over rough-paven streets. Most of the windows were dark, but now and then fantastic shadows were silhouetted against some lamp-lit blind. He watched them curiously. They moved like monstrous marionettes, and made gestures like live things. He hated them. A dull rage was in his heart. As they turned a corner a woman yelled something at them from an open door, and two men ran after the hansom for about a hundred yards. The driver beat at them with his whip.

It is said that passion makes one think in a circle. Certainly with hideous iteration the bitten lips of Dorian Gray shaped and reshaped those subtle words that dealt with soul and sense, till he had found in them the full expression, as it were, of his mood, and justified, by intellectual approval, passions that without such justification would still have dominated his temper. From cell to cell of his brain crept the one thought; and the wild desire to live, most terrible of all man's appetites, quickened into force each trembling nerve and fibre. Ugliness that had once been hateful to him because it made things real, became dear to him now for that very reason. Ugliness was the one reality. The coarse brawl, the loathsome den, the crude violence of disordered life, the very vileness of thief and outcast, were more vivid, in their intense actuality of impression, than all the gracious shapes of Art, the dreamy shadows of Song. They were what he needed for forgetfulness. In three days he would be free.

Suddenly the man drew up with a jerk at the top of a dark lane. Over the low roofs and jagged chimney-stacks of the houses rose the black masts of ships. Wreaths of white mist clung like ghostly sails to the yards.

"Somewhere about here, sir, ain't it?" he asked huskily through the trap.

Dorian started, and peered round. "This will do," he answered, and, having got out hastily, and given the driver the extra fare he had promised him, he walked quickly in the direction of the quay. Here and there a lantern gleamed at the stern of some huge merchantman. The light shook and splintered in the puddles. A red glare came from an outward-bound steamer that was coaling. The slimy pavement looked like a wet mackintosh.

He hurried on towards the left, glancing back now and then to see if he was being followed. In about seven or eight minutes he reached a small shabby house, that was wedged in between two gaunt factories. In one of the top-windows stood a lamp. He stopped, and gave a peculiar knock.

After a little time he heard steps in the passage, and the chain being unhooked. The door opened quietly, and he went in without saying a word to the squat misshapen figure that flattened itself into the shadow as he passed. At the end of the hall hung a tattered green curtain that swayed and shook in the gusty wind which had followed him in from the street. He dragged it aside, and entered a long, low room which looked as if it had once been a third-rate dancing-saloon. Shrill flaring gas-jets, dulled and distorted in the fly-blown mirrors that faced them, were ranged round the walls. Greasy reflectors of ribbed tin backed them, making quivering discs of light. The floor was covered with ochre-coloured sawdust, trampled here and there into mud, and stained with dark rings of spilt liquor. Some Malays were crouching by a little charcoal stove playing with bone counters, and showing their white teeth as they chattered. In one corner with his head buried in his arms, a sailor sprawled over a table, and by the tawdrily-painted bar that ran across one complete side stood two haggard women mocking an old man who was brushing the sleeves of his coat with an expression of disgust. "He thinks he's got red ants on him," laughed one of them, as Dorian passed by. The man looked at her in terror, and began to whimper.

At the end of the room there was a little staircase, leading to a darkened chamber. As Dorian hurried up its three ricketty steps, the heavy odour of opium met him. He heaved a deep breath, and his nostrils quivered with pleasure. When he entered, a young man with smooth yellow hair, who was bending over a lamp lighting a long thin pipe, looked up at him, and nodded in a hesitating manner.

"You here, Adrian?" muttered Dorian.

"Where else should I be?" he answered, listlessly. "None of the chaps will speak to me now."

"I thought you had left England."

"Darlington is not going to do anything. My brother paid the bill at last. George doesn't speak to me either... I don't care," he added, with a sigh. "As long as one has this stuff, one doesn't want friends. I think I have had too many friends."

Dorian winced, and looked round at the grotesque things that lay in such fantastic postures on the ragged mattresses. The twisted limbs, the gaping mouths, the staring lustreless eyes, fascinated him. He knew in what strange heavens they were suffering, and what dull hells were teaching them the secret of some new joy. They were better off than he was. He was prisoned in thought. Memory, like a horrible malady, was eating his soul away. From time to time he seemed to see the eyes of Basil Hallward looking at him. Yet he felt he could not stay. The presence of Adrian Singleton troubled him. He wanted to be where no one would know who he was. He wanted to escape from himself.

"I am going on to the other place," he said, after a pause.

"On the wharf?"

"Yes."

"That mad-cat is sure to be there. They won't have her in this place now."

Dorian shrugged his shoulders. "I am sick of women who love one. Women who hate one are much more interesting. Besides, the stuff is better."

"Much the same."

"I like it better. Come and have something to drink. I must have something."

"I don't want anything," murmured the young man.

"Never mind."

Adrian Singleton rose up wearily, and followed Dorian to the bar. A half-caste, in a ragged turban and a shabby ulster, grinned a hideous greeting as he thrust a bottle of brandy and two tumblers in front of them. The women sidled up, and began to chatter. Dorian turned his back on them, and said something in a low voice to Adrian Singleton.

A crooked smile, like a Malay crease, writhed across the face of one of the women. "We are very proud to-night," she sneered.

"For God's sake don't talk to me," cried Dorian, stamping his foot on the ground. "What do you want? Money? Here it is. Don't ever talk to me again."

Two red sparks flashed for a moment in the woman's sodden eyes, then flickered out, and left them dull and glazed. She tossed her head, and raked the coins off the counter with greedy fingers. Her companion watched her enviously.

"It's no use," sighed Adrian Singleton. "I don't care to go back. What does it matter? I am quite happy here."

"You will write to me if you want anything, won't you?" said Dorian, after a pause.

"Perhaps."

"Good-night, then."

"Good-night," answered the young man, passing up the steps, and wiping his parched mouth with a handkerchief.

Dorian walked to the door with a look of pain in his face. As he drew the curtain aside a hideous laugh broke from the painted lips of the woman who had taken his money. "There goes the devil's bargain!" she hiccoughed, in a hoarse voice.

"Curse you!" he answered, "don't call me that."

She snapped her fingers. "Prince Charming is what you like to be called, ain't it?" she yelled after him.

The drowsy sailor leapt to his feet as she spoke, and looked wildly round. The sound of the shutting of the hall door fell on his ear. He rushed out as if in pursuit.

Dorian Gray hurried along the quay through the drizzling rain. His meeting with Adrian Singleton had strangely moved him, and he wondered if the ruin of that young life was really to be laid at his door, as Basil Hallward had said to him with such infamy of insult. He bit his lip, and for a few seconds his eyes grew sad. Yet, after all, what did it matter to him? One's days were too brief to take the burden of another's errors on one's shoulders. Each man lived his own life, and paid his own price for living it. The only pity was one had to pay so often for a single fault. One had to pay over and over again, indeed. In her dealings with man Destiny never closed her accounts.

There are moments, psychologists tell us, when the passion for sin, or for what the world calls sin, so dominates a nature, that every fibre of the body, as every cell of the brain, seems to be instinct with fearful impulses. Men and women at such moments lose the freedom of their will. They move to their terrible end as automatons move. Choice is taken from them, and conscience is either killed, or, if it lives at all, lives but to give rebellion its fascination, and disobedience its charm. For all sins, as theologians weary not of reminding us, are sins of disobedience, When that high spirit, that morning-star of evil, fell from heaven, it was as a rebel that he fell.

Callous, concentrated on evil, with stained mind and soul hungry for rebellion, Dorian Gray hastened on, quickening his step as he went, but as he darted aside into a dim archway that had served him often as a short cut to the ill-famed place where he was going, he felt himself suddenly seized from behind, and before he had time to defend himself he was thrust back against the wall, with a brutal hand round his throat.

He struggled madly for life, and by a terrible effort wrenched the tightening fingers away. In a second he heard the click of a revolver, and saw the gleam of a polished barrel pointing straight at his head, and the dusky form of a short thick-set man facing him.

"What do you want?" he gasped.

"Keep quiet," said the man. "If you stir, I shoot you."

"You are mad. What have I done to you?"

"You wrecked the life of Sibyl Vane," was the answer, and Sibyl Vane was my sister. She killed herself. I know it. Her death is at your door. I swore I would kill you in return. For years I have sought you. I had no clue, no trace. The two people who could have described you were dead. I knew nothing of you but the pet name she used to call you. I heard it to-night by chance. Make your peace with God, for to-night you are going to die."

Dorian Gray grew sick with fear. "I never knew her," he stammered. "I never heard of her. You are mad."

"You had better confess your sin, for as sure as I am James Vane, you are going to die." There was a horrible moment. Dorian did not know what to say or do. "Down on your knees!" growled the man. "I give you one minute to make your peace – no more. I go on board tonight for India, and I must do my job first. One minute. That's all."

Dorian's arms fell to his side. Paralysed with terror, he did not know what to do. Suddenly a wild hope flashed across his brain. "Stop," he cried. "How long ago is it since your sister died? Quick, tell me!"

"Eighteen years," said the man. "Why do you ask me? What do years matter?"

"Eighteen years," laughed Dorian Gray, with a touch of triumph in his voice. "Eighteen years! Set me under the lamp and look at my face!"

James Vane hesitated for a moment, not understanding what was meant. Then he seized Dorian Gray and dragged him from the archway.

Dim and wavering as was the windblown light, yet it served to show him the hideous error, as it seemed, into which he had fallen, for the face of the man he had sought to kill had all the bloom of boyhood, all the unstained purity of youth. He seemed little more than a lad of twenty summers, hardly older, if older indeed at all, than his sister had been when they had parted so many years ago.

It was obvious that this was not the man who had destroyed her life.

He loosened his hold and reeled back. "My God, my God!" he cried, "and I would have murdered you!"

Dorian Gray drew a long breath. "You have been on the brink of committing a terrible crime, my man," he said, looking at him sternly. "Let this be a warning to you not to take vengeance into your own hands."

"Forgive me, sir," muttered James Vane. "I was deceived. A chance word I heard in that damned den set me on the wrong track."

"You had better go home and put that pistol away, or you may get into trouble," said Dorian, turning on his heel, and going slowly down the street.

James Vane stood on the pavement in horror. He was trembling from head to foot. After a little while a black shadow that had been creeping along the dripping wall, moved out into the light and came close to him with stealthy footsteps. He felt a hand laid on his arm and looked round with a start. It was one of the women who had been drinking at the bar.

"Why didn't you kill him?" she hissed out, putting her haggard face quite close to his. "I knew you were following him when you rushed out from Daly's. You fool! You should have killed him. He has lots of money, and he's as bad as bad."

"He is not the man I am looking for," he answered, "and I want no man's money. I want a man's life. The man whose life I want must be nearly forty now. This one is little more than a boy. Thank God, I have not got his blood upon my hands."

The woman gave a bitter laugh. "Little more than a boy!" she sneered. "Why, man, it's nigh on eighteen years since Prince Charming made me what I am."

"You lie!" cried James Vane.

She raised her hand up to heaven. "Before God I am telling

the truth," she cried.

"Before God?"

"Strike me dumb if it ain't so. He is the worst one that comes here. They say he has sold himself to the devil for a pretty face. It's nigh on eighteen years since I met him. He hasn't changed much since then. I have though," she added, with a sickly leer.

"You swear this?"

"I swear it," came in hoarse echo from her flat mouth. "But don't give me away to him," she whined; "I am afraid of him. Let me have some money for my night's lodging."

He broke from her with an oath, and rushed to the corner of the street, but Dorian Gray had disappeared. When he looked back, the woman had vanished also.

THE FLOWERS OF EVIL
& ARTIFICIAL PARADISE

Charles Baudelaire, *poète maudit*, the self-styled "Satanic man" whose collection *Les Fleurs du Mal* (*The Flowers Of Evil*) is marked by paeans to sexual degradation such as "The Litanies Of Satan" and "Metamorphosis Of The Vampire". Baudelaire himself revelled in a life of filth, and kept as his poetic muse a diseased mulatto prostitute.

The Flowers Of Evil is now presented in a brand new translation that vividly brings Baudelaire's masterpiece to life for the new millennium. This volume also includes key texts from Baudelaire's ARTIFICIAL PARADISE, his notorious examination of the effects of intoxication by alcohol and drugs. In "On Wine And Hashish", "Get Drunk" and "The Poem Of Hashish", Baudelaire brilliantly evokes the agony and ecstasy of addiction.

With an introductory essay by Guillaume Apollinaire, published for the first time in English.